# NO ESCAPE from WAR

**New York Times & USA Today Bestselling Author**

# CYNTHIA EDEN

# PROLOGUE

"Why the hell are you here?" Warren "War" Channing slapped his hands on the scarred bar top and glared at the SOB who'd just walked into *his* place. Last call had been over an hour ago, and he was damn well ready to call it a night. Even if he hadn't been ready to close, there was no way he'd want to serve this particular jackass.

Dylan Nelson yanked at the too-tight collar of his fancy dress shirt. "We need to talk."

"You need to get your ass out of my bar." Did this jerk have any idea how much self-control War was exerting by not immediately jumping across the bar and plowing his fist into Dylan's weak jaw? Knocking the guy out because he'd been the fool responsible for War's breakup with—

"I want to hire you."

"Get. The. Fuck. Out." War couldn't be clearer than that.

Beads of sweat dotted Dylan's forehead. "Look, it's about Rose—"

The expression on War's face must have stopped him. Dylan gulped and backed up a step, but he didn't leave.

Why was the dumbass staying?

"I get that you don't like me," Dylan rushed to say.

*Oh, you think?*

"You probably want to kick my ass."

Absolutely. "The thought has crossed my mind a time or twenty." And it sure was appealing right then. It was like the guy was just asking for it.

"Rose—she told me that you did PI work. That was how she first met you."

*I don't want him saying her name.* Because when Dylan said her name, it reminded War of just how bad the breakup with Rose had been.

He'd fallen fast and hard. Huge mistake. Major. But when it came to Rose Shadow, War hadn't exactly been sane. Lust, blind need—they'd taken over for him. She'd gotten under his skin, addicted him, then wrecked his world. "I'm not talking about her," he gritted out. *Sure as hell not with you.*

Dylan took another quick step back. "She's in trouble," he blurted.

War tensed. Then he leapt over the bar.

"Oh, Jesus." Dylan ran a shaking hand over his face. "Please don't break my nose. You know the business I'm in. I need my face. I'm a people person."

War's hands fisted.

"I wouldn't be here if I wasn't desperate. *Desperate.* But Rose—"

Warren growled.

"Rose said you were the best! That you kept your services low key, but you were incredible.

When it came to tracking people who didn't want to be found, no one was better. I *need* you."

"It's closing time. You are getting the hell out right now." Even if War had to throw him out, an appealing option. War reached for Dylan, more than ready to mess up that perfectly pressed, too expensive shirt as he kicked the jerk out.

"She needs you!"

War's hands froze. "I'm pretty sure I am the last man Rose needs. She made that clear."

Dylan's pale eyes darted over his face. "You're mad at her?"

"We fucking broke up, moron. I'm sure you remember."

Dylan licked his lips. "I, ah, thought she cleared up all of—no, I can see that she did not." He winced. "Look, man, it's bad. It has to be bad, or I wouldn't be here."

"Rose is in trouble? Hardly a newsflash. She's *always* in trouble. The woman thrives on it." She was a reporter. If she didn't find trouble and tell the world about it, then Rose considered that a slow news day. His fingers clenched in the fabric of Dylan's shirt. *Hello, wrinkles.* "Go find someone else who gives a shit—"

"She's going to be arrested!" Dylan's voice notched up and cracked.

War's head cocked. "Say that again." Because he'd liked what he heard.

"She's going to be thrown in jail. Cops are looking for her. I got a tip—you know, I, um, I'm connected and get insider info. Part of my job and I—"

"Stop the rambling. Get back to Rose."

"She's tied to some serious crimes." His pale blue eyes darted to and from War's, as if he couldn't quite manage to hold War's stare. "But you know Rose, she is good at staying off-grid when she wants to do it."

Oh, he knew Rose, all right. Biblically.

"She's missing. The cops are looking for her, but you can find her before they do. And if you do...look, the station wants this handled properly."

He was sure the news station wanted the situation handled in a way that was PR positive for them. And in a way that would give them the biggest scoop. "What's she going to be charged with?" Vague curiosity. He figured it might be some B&E. Rose tended to be way overzealous on her cases—

"Murder."

War laughed and shoved Dylan away. "Good one." He spun back toward the bar. "You've got five seconds to get out before I stop being nice."

"Rose said you were never nice."

A shrug. When they'd been dating, he didn't remember Rose complaining about that particular trait. He figured she'd liked him a bit bad. Some women had a thing for danger. Rose was one of those women.

"Don't you care at all?" Dylan demanded. "She's being hunted. They will throw her in jail!"

A smile tugged at his lips as he imagined that sight. Beautiful, pampered, and spoiled Rose locked away...

He could almost hear the cell door swinging shut.

"I am authorized to pay you twenty grand."

His ears perked up, and War swung back around. "Bullshit."

"No, I am truly authorized to pay you that. I can transfer the money to your account right now." Dylan smoothed a hand over his short, brown hair.

War shook his head. "I was calling bullshit on Rose committing murder. She's many things, but the woman isn't a killer."

Dylan glanced around, as if he expected someone to lunge from the shadows. He didn't need to worry. They were alone. "There's...a lot of evidence," he whispered.

"Speak up," War ordered. "Can't hear you." Yes, he could. He just didn't like this SOB. Personal reasons.

Louder, Dylan said, "We have to find her before the cops do. She's probably scared and desperate."

A desperate Rose. Interesting idea.

"*You* can find her before the authorities do. Then you and I can convince her to turn herself in. We can make sure she handles this the right way."

He shouldn't. War knew he shouldn't, but this opportunity...it was just sounding too good to pass up. "Let me make sure I've got all of this straight."

Dylan swallowed. He looked as if he might pass out.

"You are going to pay me twenty grand—right now—to track down my ex. When I find her, I get to have her ass locked up in jail?" That visual was so beautifully sweet.

"Yes, yes, that's the basic plan…"

A slow smile curved War's lips. "Then you just hired yourself a PI."

# CHAPTER ONE

Things could be worse.

Rose Shadow understood that she was in a bad situation. Definitely not ideal. But things *could* be worse.

Sure...she was suspected of murder. Multiple murders. Being a suspect had *not* been part of her original plan. And she was on the run. Again, not part of the big master plan. But...

She wasn't *in* jail...yet. Wasn't even in police custody. As long as she had her freedom, she still had a chance. This was the story of an absolute lifetime. She knew it. From the very beginning, her instincts had been screaming at her. Rose was not one to ignore screaming instincts. Well, generally, she didn't ignore them.

The last time she *had* ignored her instincts, things had gone poorly. That experience had involved a devilishly handsome, ex special ops, alpha asshole named War. *War.* Seriously, as soon as she learned his nickname, she should have run.

She hadn't. She'd...kinda hopped into bed with him. Mostly because she had a weakness for bad boys with muscles for days, deep rumbling voices...and smiles that had the tendency to make her panties melt.

She'd known War would be bad for her, but she'd still been pulled to him. They'd burned bright and hot...right up until the very, very bitter end.

If he didn't currently hate her, she could certainly have used his sneaky skills to help her get out of her unfortunate situation. But the odds of War helping her—yeah, not so good. The man could hold a grudge. Then again, so could she.

She motioned toward the waitress for another round. At the waitress's nod, Rose went back to studying the small restaurant. As far as she could tell, no one was giving her a second glance. She'd picked the shadowy corner deliberately. Her back was against the wall, so she could see everyone who entered the place, but the dim lightning meant that most folks there couldn't see her. She had a meeting with one of her informants, and that meeting *should* have occurred thirty minutes ago.

Billy was late. Only Billy was *never* late. Her stomach tightened. He was one of the few people she trusted in the area. He'd promised to help her find some temporary housing while she worked the case. But with him being a no-show...

*Clink.* "Anything else?" The waitress had set the beer bottle down on the table.

Rose slid a twenty toward her. "Yeah. Is there a back way out of this place?"

With Billy being a no-show, she had to figure that something had come up. That meant their meeting spot could have been compromised. If it was compromised, she needed to find a way to slip out, fast.

The twenty vanished. "Sure thing. Go through that red door. Take a left, and you'll be out back in thirty seconds."

Perfect.

The waitress turned to walk away.

Once more, Rose's gaze swept around the old restaurant. Darted toward the—

*Oh, no.*

A familiar figure had just slipped through the entrance doors. A big, muscled guy. Six-foot-three inches and two hundred pounds of corded strength. Rose knew all of these stats not because she was magically awesome at looking at a person and guessing...but because she knew *him.*

As if her thoughts had summoned him, War Channing stood inside the old restaurant. It was a small, out-of-the-way spot. Not on the main stretch of the beach, so it wasn't a place that most tourists would visit. More for locals. War was a local, so perhaps it was a coincidence that he was there...

But as she studied him, Rose realized his body was hard with tension, and he seemed to be inspecting every face in that place. He was looking for someone, and the sinking sensation in Rose's stomach told her that someone...*it's me.*

No, it wasn't a coincidence that War was there. He was hunting—her.

She eased out a slow breath. Her hand reached up to make certain that her wig was still in place. Tonight, she was blonde. Blonde and in the shadows and, surely, he wouldn't be able to recognize her.

Maybe?

*Get the hell out.*

She eased from her chair. His gaze was currently on a woman who sat at the bar. The woman's body shape was similar to Rose's, and her dark hair was the color Rose *usually* sported. He seemed focused on that woman, so this was the perfect time for Rose to tip-toe out of there. Holding her breath, she sidled toward the red door. She pushed it open. Took a left.

*Thirty seconds. Just thirty seconds and I will be free.*

When she shoved open the back door, the scent of garbage hit her, and Rose's nose wrinkled. But she hurriedly picked up her pace and shimmied around the side of the building so that she could get to her—

"Well, well. Funny running into you here."

She nearly *ran* straight into War's massive chest.

He was standing between her and the parking lot, and he *should* have still been inside, damn him. How the hell had he moved so fast?

But Rose pasted a bright smile on her face. There wasn't much light on that side of the building. Most of the illumination came from the moon and the stars. "War!" Did that sound welcoming enough? "How are you?" She tried to sound normal. As if she hadn't been trying to run from him.

"Pretty good. Can't complain." He crossed his arms over his chest. "Aw, who the hell am I kidding? Right now, I am fucking fabulous."

*Uh, oh.* "That's great. Happy to hear that. Wonderful for you." She backed up a step. Going through War wasn't an option. He was an immovable force who substantially outweighed and outmuscled her. But running from him in the opposite direction?

She had been on the track team in high school. *All-state, baby.* She just needed a moment for him to be distracted. A few precious seconds that would give her a head start, and then she'd be gone.

"The blonde hair is new," he noted.

Indeed, it was. New and temporary.

"Got to know, Rose...do blondes have more fun?"

Considering that she was having an extremely shitty time, the answer would be a resounding no. "So far, so good." She cleared her throat. "What brings you to Finch's tonight?" Finch's...the hole-in-the-wall restaurant that should have been safe.

"I was looking for you, sweetheart."

Two things happened right then. One, her spine snapped straight. *I was looking for you.* She took those words as the threat that they were. And two, her heart started a triple-time rhythm. He'd just said *"sweetheart"* in that low, rough, and ever-so-sexy way of his. The way he'd used to say it when he was thrusting deep inside her.

She would be lying if she said he wasn't the best lover she'd ever had. He left the others in the dust.

She would also be lying if she said she wanted to ever get back with him again. She didn't. War was trouble and pain. "Do not call me that." So, yes, those were the words she snarled back at him. "Don't use endearments that we both know you don't mean."

His head tilted to the left. His "thoughtful" pose. He had several different poses. Once upon a time, she'd cared deeply for him, so she'd learned his moves. His tells. When his head cocked to the left, he was thinking about something. When his head cocked to the right, it was game on. War was about to launch an attack.

He wasn't about to attack—yet—so she had a few more moments to figure out her escape.

"Rose, you sound bitter. If I didn't know better, I would think the breakup wasn't your idea—"

"Wasn't my—" Her nostrils flared, and she caught herself right before she lunged for him. No, going toward him would be a mistake. She needed to get away. But she also couldn't let this point pass. Rose just didn't have it in her. "I'm not the one who was an asshole with trust issues. That would be *you*." Bam. Missile delivered.

His shoulders rolled back. The rolled back shoulders meant War was getting angry. Considering that Rose was more than a little angry herself, she didn't care.

"And *I'm* not the one who made out with someone else." War took a gliding step forward. He was big, but for all of his size, the man could sure move softly.

Because she was watching his sneaky movements, it took a moment for his words to register and when they did, her jaw dropped. She snapped it back up and fired, "Dylan kissed *me*. I didn't kiss him. And I shoved him back and told him that if he ever did that crap again, I would have a sexual harassment case filed against him."

"You—what?"

He was stunned. Thrown off balance. Good. This was her chance. Tears filled her eyes because what she was saying *was* true and because she was desperate, and this was her only chance. "You never gave me an opportunity to explain. You just acted. You raged. You accused. What about a little trust, War? A little faith? Would that have been too much to ask?" She whirled away from him and hunched her shoulders.

God, she still *hurt*. This man had gotten to her. Gotten past the guard that she used to keep everyone else out. Rose knew the score in this world. Only the tough survived. Trust family, no one else. Her mantra. But...

War had been different.

Or maybe she'd just wanted him to be different.

"Rose..." His hand curled around her shoulder. He was creeping closer and closer. This was it. Her chance to get away. And her chance to get a little payback. All in one lovely movement.

*Leave me, will you? Gonna break my heart in a thousand pieces?*

Her right foot angled back. With big guys like War, it was all a matter of...balance. Or rather, making him lose his balance.

"Are you telling me the truth?" he whispered.

She angled her body. "War..." Her head turned toward him just the faintest bit.

As he leaned his body toward hers...she struck. Her right foot swept hard against his ankle, and the mighty War went down with a bellow. "Go screw yourself," she snapped at him. Then she was off. Racing as fast as she could through the night. When she wanted to be fast...

Rose *was* fast.

If tears fell as she ran away, at least War couldn't see them.

\*\*\*

He'd been played by a master. War jumped up. She'd pushed him into a stinking pile of garbage, and he knew that landing spot had been deliberate. Rose was one strategic plotter. He raked God-knew-what off his shoulder and bellowed, "Rose!"

She didn't slow down. Snarling, he gave chase. His feet pounded over the ground as he flew after her. She was close to a waiting Jeep. Not her car. She always drove a convertible and it was currently sitting in her garage, but as he watched, Rose jumped into the Jeep and had the engine snarling to life. She whipped that vehicle into reverse, and gravel flew from beneath the tires. She started to shoot it forward.

War leapt into her path. His hands flew up. "Stop!" She might shove him into a pile of stinking garbage and rotting food, but he didn't think she'd run him down.

Hopefully.

The Jeep's headlights nearly blinded him.

"It's over, Rose," he yelled. She could hear him. The doors and roof of the Jeep had been removed. It was a beach town, and most of the Jeeps in the area looked that way. "I'm turning you in."

She revved the engine. "Get out of the way."

"No. You'll have to go through me because I am not moving." And she wouldn't do it. She'd give in. She'd turn off the Jeep. Get out. Maybe rage at him again. But then he'd take that ever so sweet ass of hers to jail and laugh while she made her frantic explanations to the cops and—

The wheels spun. Gravel spit into the air. And the Jeep flew *back*. She reversed through the lot like a champ as he gaped after her. Too late, he realized she was heading for the little hill that *wasn't* an exit, but a place that would still allow her to access the road. He surged after her, but by then, she had too much of a lead on him. With a happy little honk of her horn—a sound he was ninety-nine percent sure meant *screw you*—she whipped onto the street and raced away from him.

*Sonofabitch.*

His breath was heaving as he ran to the edge of the road and glowered after her...after her *and* after the license plate that he could see illuminated thanks to the lights on the back of the Jeep.

His hands slapped against his thighs. A smile stretched across his face. *Oh, sweetheart, you can run, but I will find you.*

Once he started a hunt, he never stopped.

***

She parked the Jeep in the back of the motel so that it would be hidden from anyone passing by on the road. Before going back to her little no-tell-motel, Rose had swung by Billy's place, hoping against hope that he would be there.

The house had been deserted.

So she'd been forced to return to her current lodging spot. Not directly on the beach, but rather hidden on a back bay—the spot would have to do. For now.

She couldn't leave the area. Not until she'd finished her job. Or until the job finished her. A grim possibility considering her last few days.

Sticking to the shadows, Rose made her way to room number one-oh-four. The light near the door flickered and pulsed to reveal the chipped wood along the frame. This place was far different from her beloved condo with its gulf view, and that was exactly the reason she'd taken refuge there. Until it was safe, she had to stay under the radar.

Her hand lifted for the door. She swiped the key and then slipped inside. The air conditioner was humming, even though she'd tried seven times to turn the thing off before she'd left, and the room was absolutely icy. The bored clerk at the front desk had told her he'd get a repairman in tomorrow. She'd *hoped* to be gone by that point.

Rose yanked off the blonde wig and tossed it on the little table that she knew waited close to the door. Her hair tumbled around her shoulders, and the pressure she'd felt on her head immediately eased. Her hand reached to the right as she prepared to flip on the light—

"Took you long enough to come inside," a low, growling voice said from the darkness.

A scream tore from Rose's throat, and she immediately grabbed the door to fly back outside. Terror clawed at her, and all she could think was...*he found me.* She'd tried so hard, but he'd found her. She yanked open the door, but a powerful hand shoved it closed. In the next breath, he'd spun her around to face him.

Rose immediately went to knee the intruder in the groin, but he moved too fast. He shoved one of his legs between hers as his hands clamped around her waist. "*Not happening.*" Another dark growl. Angry. Rough and—

*Wait.*

She froze with her hands hanging in the air. Her intent had been to dig her thumbs into his eyes. A vicious move, yes, but when times were desperate, one *did* vicious things to stay alive.

Except...her attacker wasn't the man she'd thought. "War?" His name emerged as a croak.

"Who the fuck else would it be?"

Who else? Oh, just the man who wanted her dead. The killer she was both hunting for and hiding from. Before she could respond, there was a frantic knock on the door behind her.

"Hey! What in the hell is happening in there?" A thick drawl coated the words. "Y'all okay?"

War leaned in close to her. The light was still off, so she couldn't see him, but she could feel him all around her. His breath blew over her cheek as he whispered, "Tell the nice man that you're fine."

"I don't feel fine," she whispered right back. "How about I tell him that? How about I tell him that some psycho broke into my motel room?"

A low, amused chuckle slipped from War. "Do it. Then he can call the cops. I'm sure you'd love that."

No, she'd hate it. He knew that, damn him. War had just called her bluff. "I'm fine!" Rose called back to the would-be rescuer on the other side of the door. "Thanks for checking. Sorry to be so loud!"

Another rap pounded against the door. "You screamed." A pause. "You alone in there?"

He obviously thought she was being threatened, and he was determined to help. Nice to know there were some good people in the world. But if this good person didn't leave soon, she was going to have serious trouble on her hands.

"My boyfriend is here," she shouted back. A shout because War was close, and she thought yelling in his ear might just get the man to back up. He didn't, so she added, just as loudly, "We got a little carried away! Sorry!" *Keep going, would-be hero. Nothing to see here.*

Rose thought she heard a grunt then the guy groused, "Keep that shit down. People are sleeping." A few moments later, Rose heard a door slam. The door on the right. Great. He was staying in the room that connected to hers.

"You can back away now," Rose informed War crisply.

"If I back away, you might try to run."

That had been precisely her plan.

"So, first, how about you give me the keys—the key to the room and the keys to the Jeep—then we'll talk about backing away."

She turned her right hand over.

He swiped the keys. "Thank you."

*Fuck you.* She bit back the retort.

"Were you going for my eyes, Rose? Such a dirty move."

"You're the one who taught me that move." When he'd been adamant that she learn how to defend herself. Only she'd never thought that she'd have to defend herself from him. Another thing she'd been wrong about.

"I taught you lots of dirty things." His voice had taken on a rougher, more sensual edge.

Even in the dark, her eyes narrowed. He wanted to be cocky? Wanted to go *there*? "I am pretty sure I taught you a thing or twenty, too, stud."

A rumble of laughter broke from him. His body pressed closer to her.

Alarm skittered through her. "Get off me."

"I'm not on you. I'm near you. I'm in front of you. Definitely not on you."

She wanted to scream, but if she did that, her helpful neighbor would probably rush back over. Then she'd have to deal with that whole bit of business again. "War..."

"Rose..."

"Turn on the lights. Let's talk about this like civilized people."

"But you know I've never been particularly civilized. I think that was one of your issues with me."

Her breath caught. "Sometimes, I liked it." Particularly in bed. Out of bed... "It was only when you became too much of an ass that I had issues."

His hand lifted. She felt it rise, felt the shift in the air, and then heard the click as he flipped on the lights. Her eyes closed and opened quickly, twice, three times, as she adjusted to the flood of illumination.

He was right in front of her. Just as tall, dark, and dangerously handsome as always. His skin was golden from all the time he spent in the sun. His hair was dark and thick, shoving back from his forehead. His face was planes and angles— sexy and strong. Hard jaw. Lickable lips. And eyes so very deep. His eyes could be a warm, sensual brown, or they could flash with ice-cold darkness, all depending on his mood. Right then, his eyes were...

She swallowed. "What are you going to do to me?"

"Take that sweet ass to jail." He tucked her keys in his back pocket. Then his hands rose and pressed to the door behind her, caging her between his body and the wood. "You're in trouble, sweetheart."

"Don't call me that." Her heart was pounding too fast again. Actually, her heart had been racing ever since she'd found him waiting in her room. Just *how* had he found her in that motel, anyway? Rose had tried to be so careful. She'd kept her phone off as much as possible because she feared being tracked. "Don't use words that you don't mean. I'm not dear to you so don't use an *endearment*."

"Fair enough." He gave her a half smile. The same smile that had once made her heart jump.

Of course, her crazy heart still jumped.

"I have something else I was hoping to use on you, anyway." His gaze swept over her face. "How are you still this beautiful?" His voice had turned into a rasp. All sensual and rough. "You know, I think I *almost* missed you."

She had missed him. She'd cried over the jerk. Had to bury her sorrows in her favorite cookie dough ice cream. Then she'd made herself move the hell on. If he didn't trust her, if he didn't want to fight for what they had, if he didn't have faith in *them*...the man didn't deserve her or her pain.

"Almost," War continued as he *finally* dropped his hands and took a step away from her. "Right up until the moment when you shoved me into a pile of garbage. Not a cool move, sweet— Rose."

Her chin notched up. "If you're expecting an apology, you have the wrong woman." He didn't get it. She was fighting for her life. If she had to fight dirty, so be it. "You don't understand what is happening here. And I don't even understand *why* you are here!"

"Oh, that's simple. I'm here...because I'm hunting you."

She sucked in a sharp breath. She'd feared that would be the case.

"I was *hired* to hunt you. To find you. To turn you over to the cops."

Frantic, Rose shook her head. "No, no, please, War, give me a chance to explain!" Talk about a nightmare situation. "It's not what you think! I'm not—"

"If you're expecting me to believe your lies, you have the wrong man."

Ice covered her heart. She'd never lied to him.

His hand reached behind his back.

Rose tensed.

"Remember when I said I had something else I planned to use on you?"

Fear flooded through her. "War, *don't*."

War lifted the handcuffs he'd just pulled out. "Guess what? I think these are going to fit you *perfectly*."

# CHAPTER TWO

He'd never seen fear on Rose's face before. He'd seen lots of other things. Happiness. Pleasure. Pain. But not fear.

War hadn't liked it when he saw the pain. The pain had been there on the last night that they'd been together, the night she'd left him. And right now, he sure as hell wasn't liking the fear he could see, either.

"I'm not going to hurt you," he said. Rose should know better than that. "I'm just going to haul you to jail."

She licked her lips. Her delectable, bow-shaped, ever so bitable lips. Lips that felt like heaven against his. Lips that still made their way into his dreams. *She* made her way into his dreams on far too many nights. With the tumble of dark hair that skimmed her shoulders, her emerald eyes—a gorgeous green that normally sparkled with her emotions—and her smooth, creamy skin, she was a stunner. He'd been hooked on her long before they met in person. Embarrassing to admit, but he'd always tuned in for the nightly news just so he could watch her. A fucking crush. Then she'd walked into his bar...

And he'd been a goner. Two days after meeting her in person, he'd had her in his bed. He'd planned to keep her there.

But that shit hadn't happened.

Now she was staring at him with her eyes all stark and scared, her lower lip was trembling, and if he didn't know better... "I'm not the freaking wolf."

Her eyes became even bigger.

"Stop looking at me like I'm going to bite you," he growled. Okay. Growling probably wasn't the way to reassure her, and he *had* nibbled on her in the past, but those had been sensual, heat-of-the-moment-type bites.

"I'm looking at you like you're the crazy guy who just threatened to *cuff* me!"

"Oh, come on." The words burst from him. "Like I haven't cuffed you before."

Heat immediately stained her cheeks. "That was different. And it was *one* time."

It had been one hot as hell time. He wasn't going to point out that she'd enjoyed that particular instance of being cuffed...because he knew she wasn't going to have fun tonight. "It's just temporary. I'll slap a cuff on your wrist, then one on mine. It's to make sure you don't try to ditch me again."

"I assure you, I *will* try to ditch you."

He grunted. "I figured as much." The cuffs felt cold in his grip. Why the hell hadn't he slapped one on her yet? What was he waiting for? "Once we're at the police station, I'll take it off."

"I can't go to the police station."

"You're a person of interest in a murder investigation." His head cocked to the left.

Her eyes narrowed on him.

"Two murders, actually," he clarified. "So, yes, you will be going to the police station."

"You don't believe I killed anyone, do you?"

"I think you need to talk to the cops." He reached for her hand. Time to cuff her.

*"Don't."* Breathy. Desperate.

He'd rarely seen Rose be desperate. Come to think of it, this might be the first time he'd ever heard that particular note in her voice.

"You don't get what's at play here, War."

"Sure I do. Twenty grand is at play."

"What?"

"Twenty. Grand." A nod. "That's how much Dylan is paying me to bring you in. Remember Dylan? Oh, I am sure you—"

"Don't be an ass. We both know I remember my producer. But why is he paying you anything?"

"Because he is worried about you." Instead of snapping the cuff around her delicate wrist, his hand lifted, and the back of his knuckles slid over her silken cheek. "Another dumbass who got obsessed with you."

"You were never obsessed with me."

His hand fell. "Of course not."

"Dylan isn't, either. He knows nothing will happen between us. I've made it abundantly clear—as I told you at Finch's." Her breath huffed out. "Why on earth would he go to you if he was worried about me? He is aware that you and I are no longer together."

"Right. Not together. Not at all." She smelled delicious. Like some kind of fancy cream that he wanted to lap up. "But you must have been singing my praises at the station because he said you told him I was the best PI in town. That I could find anyone." He wiggled his brows at her. "Not that you were wrong. Case in point, I found you."

"You are being a dick. This is serious, War!"

"I don't remember laughing." Certainly not when she'd shoved him in the stinking pile of garbage. Which reminded him...she smelled delicious, and he probably smelled like shit. No wonder she kept huffing and twitching that cute little button nose of hers. "Your producer wants you brought in—he wants it to look like you're willing and cooperating with the cops."

"Right. Because being brought to the station in handcuffs just screams cooperation."

He shrugged. He still hadn't put them on her. He also still had his body way too close to hers. "You shouldn't have run." That part he just didn't get. "I'm not talking about running from me at the restaurant, though you shouldn't have done that, either. But you shouldn't have run from the crime scenes." No, he didn't believe she was a killer. Those vics had been strangled, and he could not imagine Rose doing that to another person. "You should have cleared things up, you should have—"

"You have no idea what is happening." Her words rushed out. "I had to run. I had to hide. If I hadn't, I'd be dead."

For a stunned moment, War didn't move. Not so much as a muscle or flicker of an eyelid.

"Did you hear me?" Impatience sharpened her voice. "Or do you just not care?"

War shook his head. "Playing your games, are you? Nice try, but it won't work. You won't get killed at the police station. You won't—"

"I'm tracking a serial killer. It started out as the biggest case of my career, but it has spiraled into something altogether different. I'm tracking him, but he's tracking me, too. If he finds me, I am dead."

"That's not fucking going to happen." An immediate denial. He shoved back his shoulders.

And just like that...hope flashed on her face.

*Shit. She played me. She—*

"It won't happen if you help me," Rose said excitedly. "You and your special ops skills—I need them. I mean, I need you. You can help me."

He slapped the cuff around her wrist.

"Wait! Stop! What are you doing?"

He thought it was obvious. He tugged her across the room. Toward the bathroom. He tested the towel bar. Found it surprisingly secure. Satisfied that it would hold her, War snapped the second cuff around that bar.

"You said you'd cuff me to you! Not to the bathroom!" Rose wailed.

"Shh." He put one finger to his lips. "You don't want our nosey next door neighbor coming in."

Once more, her cheeks were flushed a dark red. "I ask for your help, and in return, you cuff me in the bathroom? The breakup was bad, War, but was it this bad?"

He wasn't touching that one. "I'm going to my car. I have a change of clothes in there. Since *someone* pushed me into a pile of garbage, I smell to high heaven. I'll get the clothes, then shower—"

"What? Are you planning to shower with me cuffed in here?"

He winked. "Not like it isn't something you haven't seen before."

*"War."*

"Relax. I'll be gone for two minutes, tops. Then when I come back, I'll blindfold you. That way, you won't see my buff, naked body."

*"I asked for your help! And this is how you respond—"*

He brought his face down in front of hers. So close that their mouths were barely an inch apart. "I don't always think clearly when you are near. With that in mind, I am taking two minutes." *To get my sanity and control in place.* "I'll be back. Then we'll figure out what our next step will be." Shit. That last part had been a screw up, and he knew she'd caught it—

"Our?" Rose repeated as her eyes lit up.

He'd always gotten lost in those incredible eyes of hers.

"Are you going to help me?" Rose pushed. She licked her lower lip.

His cock shoved against the front of his jeans. Oh, the memory of that tongue of hers. Her lips. Her mouth on him—

*Get your control.* "Try not to scream while I'm gone. Really don't want to have to deal with our neighbor." Then he yanked his gaze away from her. Marched out of the bathroom. He took the motel room key with him. And he pulled the door shut behind him.

For a moment, he just stood there, sucking in some deep breaths.

*Rose.*

The woman could still get beneath his skin. She could pull him in and put him under her spell with barely any effort. She was on the run, and he *should* have already been taking her to the cops. Instead, he was actually going to listen to her story...

Surely, though, she was wrong. Rose wasn't the target of some crazed killer. No way.

Right?

War stalked toward his car, aware of a thickening knot of tension in his gut. He pulled out his phone and called a buddy he knew, a man he could trust. The call was answered on the second ring. "Hey, Odin." War didn't bother to identify himself. "I need a major favor."

\*\*\*

This was insane. Rose twisted her body, brought her foot up to push against the tiled wall, and then she heaved with all of her might against the towel rod. The thing must be freaking cemented in place because it did not budge.

Her breath panted in and out as she strained. She couldn't believe that War had cuffed her in the bathroom. Cuffed her and then walked away. Knowing War as she did, Rose figured he had probably just left to make some phone call. Maybe to call the cops or Dylan or *someone* who would make this situation even worse for her.

She'd asked for the man's help. Been desperate and sincere. In response, he'd dumped her in the bathroom. Obviously, any tender emotions that he'd had for her were long gone. Dead and buried. *If* he'd ever really cared at all. Maybe it had just been about the sex for him.

Her foot slipped down the wall. She brought it right back up and ground her teeth together as she heaved once more.

The sex had been fantastic. But for her, it had been so much more than just—

*Creak.*

Her breath huffed out as she heard the faint sound of the motel's door opening. "Already back? I don't think that was even two minutes." She let her foot flop back to the floor. She took a step to the side so she could peer into the main area of the room. From that spot, she actually had a clear view all the way across the motel room and she could see that...

*The door is shut.*

The door leading outside was still closed, and she didn't spy War in the room.

She inched forward, moving as far as the cuff would allow her to go. She'd very distinctly heard that creaking sound, and yes, old buildings creaked, but Rose was getting a very, very bad feeling about this situation.

*It wasn't the front door.*

She stretched and managed to poke her head out of the bathroom. It was a good thing the bathroom was the size of a shoebox or she'd never have been able to do it and—

A door was opening. *Not* the main door to the motel room, though. The door that connected her room to the one next to it—*that* door was opening. It was creaking as the hinges shifted.

She couldn't move.

*Maybe it's the would-be hero! Maybe you can convince him to help you. Maybe—*

Maybe not. Because the man coming through that connecting door was wearing a black mask over his face. One of those creepy morph-type masks that she'd seen kids wear on Halloween. It hid his entire face, but she knew those masks were designed so that he could see straight through it.

You didn't wear a mask when you were the hero who'd come to help a screaming woman. You wore a mask when you were the bad guy.

She flew back into the bathroom. Too late. She'd seen the mask angle toward her.

*Oh, God. Oh, God.* "War!" Rose screamed. "War!" Where in the hell was he when she needed him?

The intruder—wearing all back—lunged for the bathroom.

Rose couldn't run. The stupid cuff held her in place, and she didn't have a weapon on her. She couldn't even reach for anything in the bathroom that might help her.

She was trapped.

And he was closing in.

*"War!"* A desperate shriek.

The guy surged toward her. Rose kicked out at him as hard as she could.

\*\*\*

"I am totally over her," War snapped into his phone. "Look, I just want to find out more about the cases. Could you do that for me? Get to tappity-tap-tapping on the computer or call in some favors for me, but get me the case files so I can—" He broke off. He'd sure thought he'd just heard...

"So you can—what?" Odin Shaw demanded. "Do not leave me in suspense. But I think I pretty much know how the sentence ends. It goes something like... 'So I can get the woman back in my bed again by playing hero for her and—'"

"I heard it again."

"Heard what?"

War was already surging away from his parked car. "I think she's screaming." He hung up the phone. Shoved it into his pocket and flew back for room one-oh-four. When he got there, he grabbed for the door.

*Still locked.*

His hand shoved the key toward—

*Stop.* His mental order. He'd been sure that he heard Rose scream, and he'd acted on instinct as he hurtled for her. But...what if this was a trick?

What if Rose was trying to get the guy next door to help her?

What if she was just jerking War around?

What if—

Fuck it. *What if she really needs me?* He shoved open the door. "Rose! If this is some kind of con, this shit is not funny—"

Some SOB in head-to-toe black was in the bathroom. War could see his figure as he struggled with—

*Rose.*

"Get the hell away from her!" War roared as he leapt across that room. He reached the bastard, and War locked his hands around the sonofabitch's shoulders. War yanked the guy back and shoved him in the outer room, toward the bed. He had a flash of the morph mask that the man wore. It completely covered his face and head.

Rose grabbed at the towel that had been locked around her neck. She could only grab with one hand because the other was still cuffed to the towel bar.

*He'd been strangling her!*

"Baby?" War sank to his knees before her. He threw the towel aside with shaking fingers. "Are you okay?"

Her eyes were huge. Her face flushed. She nodded quickly even as a tear slid down her cheek.

That tear put him in a killing rage. War jumped back to his feet. That bastard would pay. He whirled around.

"War, no!" A quick croak from Rose. "Don't leave me!"

The attacker wasn't in the motel room. The front door hung open—War hadn't shut it when he'd rushed inside. He flew toward that door.

"*War.*" Rose's desperate voice. "I don't...don't know that he's working alone. I'm cuffed."

Tension burned in his blood. He wanted to give chase so badly.

"Get me out of the cuffs. Don't l-leave me." A plea.

In an instant, he was at her side. He yanked out the key to the cuffs and freed her wrist. His fingers slid over her skin. Her wrist was red and swollen, and he knew she'd been fighting desperately to get free when that asshole attacked her.

Outside, he heard the screech of tires. Swearing, he curled his fingers with Rose's, and together, they raced for that still open door. By the time he got to the lot, he could smell exhaust from the fleeing vehicle, but he couldn't see the car. It was long gone.

*Sonofabitch.*

"T-told you," Rose whispered as she tried to tug her hand free of his grip. "Someone is after me. Someone...other than you..."

Her voice was weak. *Because some prick just tried to kill her!* He let her fingers go, but only so he could use his hand to tip back her head and study her neck. "We're getting you to a hospital."

"No."

*No?* "Uh, hell, yes, we are. You need to be checked out. You need—"

"I need to get somewhere safe. Then I need to come up with a plan." With each word she spoke, her voice seemed to become a little stronger. But she still had tear tracks on her cheeks, dammit. "I need to find him. To *stop* him."

"We're calling the cops." He yanked out his phone.

Her fingers closed around his wrist. "War, please. *Please.*"

He stilled.

"Do you want me to beg? Because I am."

He'd never wanted that.

Okay. Fine. One fantasy. One small fantasy of her begging to come back to him because he was freaking human. But he had never, ever wanted this. He'd *never* wanted some piece of shit to hurt her. And War was ready to *kill*.

"There is a whole lot involved here. I-I can't go to the cops. They have evidence that makes me look guilty. I have to find the man who attacked me. Have to stop h-him. *Please*," she said again, and the word tore at the heart that War had thought he'd locked away from her. "I need your help. Forty-eight hours. Give me that much. Pl—"

"You don't need to ask again. We'll make a deal." They were making a deal. The deal was...*she doesn't leave my sight*. Because he was not—not ever freaking again—going to rush in and discover her battling for her life.

His heart couldn't take that shit.

Her shoulders sagged. "Thank you."

She shouldn't thank him. Just like she didn't need to plead with him. They'd cover all of that soon enough. But for now... "You stay at my side."

"What?"

"No running. No trying to get away. I will give you forty-eight hours, but I want to make sure I won't be chasing after you the whole time. Give me your word. Right now. Then we'll start this hunt."

Her breath shuddered out. "I give you my word. Forty-eight hours, and I won't run."

Damn straight.

"Come on." He threaded his fingers with hers and hurried back to her room. A quick glance at the place showed him the connecting door hung open. Jaw locking, he headed straight for that room. Maybe the jerk who'd been in there had left some clues behind.

But...

When he went inside, nothing was disturbed. The bed was neatly made. The desk empty. The bathroom appeared not to have been touched. The toilet paper was still in that weird little triangle the way it always was when new people checked into a room.

It looked like no one had been in the room at all.

But someone *had* been there...

"I don't think that man who heard me scream earlier wanted to help," Rose murmured.

No, he'd wanted to kill her. *That* was why he'd asked if she was alone. He'd wanted to get to her while she was vulnerable. He'd stayed close and waited until War walked away, then he'd attacked.

War's phone rang, vibrating in his pocket, and by the heavy metal ringtone, he knew he was getting a call from Odin. For the moment, War ignored his friend. He rushed with Rose to the small office at the front of the motel. When the desk clerk saw War coming, a satisfied smile tilted his lips. "Found your lady, did you?" Then he got a look at Rose. He whistled. "I would've wanted to surprise her, too..."

War slapped his free hand down on the counter. "Who the fuck was in the room next door?"

The man jumped back. Behind the slightly askew lenses of his glasses, his gray eyes widened. His pale skin became even paler. "I-I—"

"Who was in the room?"

"What room?" He blinked.

"Ahem. One-oh-six," Rose supplied helpfully. Her voice was a little husky, but no longer croaky.

The desk clerk squinted at her. "I know you."

"One-oh-six," War snapped. This guy was trying patience War did not have. Rage and adrenaline burned through him. *Rose could have been killed while I was less than twenty feet away.*

Instead of giving War the info he needed, the clerk was still lost looking at Rose. "Haven't I seen you somewhere before?"

Yeah. On the news. They didn't have time for this crap. War moved his body to shield Rose. "You've never seen her." He grabbed the guy by the shirtfront. "I will not repeat my question again."

"Th-there's no one! No one in that room! Not that room, not any rooms on that side—just you and your lady! That's it!"

"Do not lie to me," War warned, voice low and lethal. "That would be a fatal mistake."

"Oh, shit. Oh, *shit*." The man—his name tag identified him as Todd—began to shake. "No one is there, I swear it! I didn't assign that room to anyone!"

"Who did you tell about her?"

"What?" His face scrunched.

"Someone came here asking questions about her. You gave that someone her room number. I want to know who it was. Describe him to me. Tell me everything."

But Todd shook his head. "You."

"Me—what?"

"You're the only one who came asking questions! Just *you*. You gave me a twenty for her room number."

"Twenty dollars?" Rose piped in to say. "Really? That's it?"

Jaw locking, War kept his glare on Todd. "Someone tried to kill my fiancée tonight."

"Now I'm your fiancée?" Rose inquired. "Good to know."

He ignored Rose. For the moment. "I take someone attacking her *very* personally. If I find out you are lying to me, *Todd,* I will be back. I will make your life hell, I promise you."

"I think I'm gonna be sick." Todd was looking a little green. "I don't like confrontations. Could you let me—"

War shoved Todd back. "He attacked her. He could have killed her. Think about that the next time you give up a woman's room number for twenty dollars."

"But I only told *you!*"

"Yeah, but for all you knew, I could have been the murdering asshole." He wasn't going to get anything from Todd. The man was scared to death, and War didn't think he was lying.

*But I'll still dig into his life.*

He shoved a card at the guy. "You think of something else, you remember seeing someone else, you call this number, got it?"

A white card with a number embossed in black.

Todd nodded quickly. The card vanished in his sweaty grip.

War spun back to Rose. "Come on. We should get the hell out of here."

Her brows climbed. She looked back at Todd, then toward War. "Fine." She headed outside with him without another word. She immediately turned her body toward the Jeep.

"No, sweetheart. We're taking my ride." His hands closed around her shoulders, and he angled her toward his car, a beast of a classic Impala from '67 that he'd spent countless hours lovingly restoring after he'd done his last mission as a SEAL.

"What? Why?"

"Because the jackass who was in your room probably knows what you were driving. We have to assume that." He wasn't about to take any chances. "Maybe he was at the restaurant earlier. Maybe he saw you there and followed you. However he figured it out, the Jeep stays, and you come with me."

He thought she'd argue. He was ready for arguments. But Rose just grimly nodded, and that worried the hell out of him. *She's still afraid.*

"I hid my bag under the passenger seat. Just let me get it, all right?"

He got it for her. Then he unlocked the passenger side of his ride and wrenched open the Impala's door even as he mentally gave an apology to his baby for being so rough with her handles. "Get in the car," he told Rose.

She slid inside. Looked up at him. "Thank you."

"I haven't done anything yet." He shut the door, using much more care. He stored Rose's small bag in the trunk. Moments later, he was in the driver's seat and cranking the engine. It purred like the perfect machine it was.

Her fingers touched his hand. "You saved my life. If you hadn't come in when you did, he would have killed me."

That was not the visual War wanted in his head. Rage was still twisting inside of him, getting thicker and hotter. "If I hadn't left you cuffed in the bathroom, you would have at least had a fighting chance." His head turned so he could stare at her. "I'm sorry."

Her lips pressed together. "Are we...friends again?"

"We were never friends." Things had always been too hot and too complicated between them. "Friends don't want to constantly fuck each other." He reversed the car.

"Oh."

She didn't deny the constant desire. Good to know it had been mutual.

"If we're not friends, then what are we?" Rose asked him.

His lips parted. *I'm the man who will stand between you and any damn threat out there. And you—you are—*

"War? What are we?"

"Hell if I know." He slanted her a fast glance. "Buckle your seatbelt."

Her fingers slid away. Fumbling, she buckled the seatbelt.

"You're going to tell me everything. You're going to explain to me exactly what has happened and why the hell we aren't going to the cops after that jackass just tried to kill you."

"You might not like my explanations."

"I already figured that out." The Impala shot onto the street. Slid through the darkness. "But you're still going to tell me everything."

"Okay..." A pause. "I get the forty-eight hours, though, don't I? You promised, and I will pay you whatever you want."

He didn't remember promising. But... "You get forty-eight hours." And in terms of payment... "Whatever I want?"

"Don't be dirty, War. I'm not sleeping with you for payment."

"Sex between us would never be about payment. Sweet—" He caught himself before he called her sweetheart. "Rose, you know that, for us, sex is always about pleasure."

"Just drive the damn car." Disgruntled.

"Yes, ma'am."

# CHAPTER THREE

"Why on earth are we *here?*" Rose wondered if she sounded as nervous as she felt. She certainly felt very, very nervous. When War had promised to help her hunt, she had thought they would actually...hunt. As in, hit the streets running as they tried to track down the man who'd attacked her. Instead, War had brought her to his place. A place that held far too many memories for her.

"We're here because I want to check you out."

"I don't need checking out. I'm fine."

He grunted.

Then he reached for her hand.

She jerked it back. "What are you doing?"

His home—an old beach house that he'd bought with plans to renovate—seemed to rock gently on its heavy wooden stilts. They were on the home's screened-in porch, a porch that gave them a killer view of the Gulf of Mexico as the waves pounded onto the shore. It was after midnight, and the full moon glowed down on the beach.

They'd made love on that beach. Beneath the moon. As the waves crashed against the shore.

They'd made love on the hammock that hung on the porch. Swaying back and forth as pleasure pounded through them both.

They'd made love on the floor of his den. In his massive king bed. In the shower that he'd renovated. They'd—

"I want to take a look at your wrist. And, jeez, what are you thinking about right now? Your body has gone all tense on me."

"I'm thinking," she huffed out, "that this is a colossal waste of time. I don't need you to check me out. We need to be out hunting. Pounding the pavement. That's what you promised to do."

"I'm not hunting until I get the full story. To get that story, you need a safe haven. This is it." He motioned vaguely around them. "Not like people will expect you to be bunking at your ex's place. You should be good here, since coming back to me is the last thing most people would figure you'd do."

He wasn't wrong. But she didn't like being surrounded by all the memories there. Everywhere she looked, Rose saw *them*.

"You think I don't know you're dead on your feet? You did a great job with the makeup. You're gorgeous, as always, but I can see the shadows beneath your eyes. You need to crash. You can do that here. Talk to me. Tell me everything. Then sleep. When you wake up, we'll find your attacker."

Suspicion immediately had her spine straightening. "You mean when I wake up, I'll find you gone as you hunt him on your own and leave me behind."

He didn't deny the charge.

"No." Rose stepped toe-to-toe with him. Her head tipped back as she stared up at him, or tried to stare at him. The porch was dark, and he was in shadows which meant seeing his expression was hard. "You are not leaving me behind."

"I didn't plan to leave you. I said I wanted you at my side, remember? You're the one who just jumped to the wrong conclusion. Tsk. Tsk. Shouldn't do that. Because despite your best efforts, you don't know what I'm thinking."

No, she'd never known. Not until the end. When he'd told her what he really thought. She sucked in a breath, remembering the pain, and started to slide back—

"What?" A quick demand. "What just hurt you?"

*You did.* "I can't see anything out here. Let's go inside." Mostly so she could try to put distance between them. But when they got inside, and he flipped on the lights...

*The floor. The couch.* They'd made love so often, and she'd been so happy and— "Is that a picture of me?" She gaped at the framed photo on the end table. Then Rose marched toward it.

He beat her to the punch and flipped it down, face first. "Been doing lots of work at the bar. Renovating the area upstairs. That's where I've been mostly living the last few weeks. Haven't gotten out here much so I haven't had a chance to, ah, clean out the place."

Clean out...Right. That was code for he hadn't had the chance to throw away the picture of them. He was explaining so she wouldn't be confused and get the wrong idea about how he might feel. He shouldn't have worried. She knew exactly how he felt. *"It's been fun. The sex was great. But it's time for you to get the hell out, Rose."* His voice would haunt her late at night.

"You probably still have some clothes here." Said casually. "Maybe a toothbrush. Not a big deal. Considering everything that is happening, you're probably lucky to have that stuff here."

She sank onto the couch. The cushions were soft and thick, and she wanted to curl her legs beneath her body and just roll up into a sad ball. Everything was so out of control. "I'm scared." The confession slipped from her. And, yes, after her admission, she kicked off her shoes and curled up. Why the hell not? She was bone tired and curling up felt good.

He stared down at her. "You don't need to be scared."

A bitter laugh broke from Rose. "I have a serial killer chasing after me." She peered up at him. "A serial killer," she enunciated slowly. "Not some wanna-be thug. But an actual monster who has a string of bodies behind him. And I'm his next target. He's not going to stop until he gets me."

A muscle flexed along War's hard jaw. He leaned down, and his hands pressed to the cushions around her. "You don't need to be scared," War repeated softly.

Her breath caught.

"Do you think for one second that I will let him get his hands on you again? If I'd known about him in that motel room, if I'd known the truth, I would never have left you. Dammit, Rose, why didn't you come to me as soon as you were in trouble?"

Why? She'd thought that was obvious. "Because you hate me."

He jerked back as if he'd been electrocuted. "What?"

"You told me to get out of your life. That you never wanted to see me again. You said I couldn't be trusted, and that our time together was a waste."

He scrubbed a hand over his jaw. "I said all that shit?"

"All that and plenty more." Words that were burned into her memory.

"I was...upset."

She snorted.

His hand dropped. "Why the hell have I always found that sound sexy?"

It—

"Correction, why the hell do I find every single thing about you sexy?"

Her lips pressed together.

"I was drunk and upset that night, and I said things I didn't mean."

No, she wouldn't buy that excuse. "First, I've never seen you drunk. You drink, yes, but you don't go past your limits." That was War. Always in complete and utter control. "And two—I'm sure you meant everything you said. I could see it in your eyes." She did not want to walk down this particular path again. Especially not when she felt weak and vulnerable and all shaky on the inside. "Look, someone tried to kill me tonight." She rubbed her fingers over her throat. "Can we skip the dreaded walk down memory lane? You told me to hit the road. I hit it."

"You walked away without looking back."

Seriously? "What did you expect me to do?" Now pride had her angling up her chin. "For your information..." In case he was under the wrong impression. "There are plenty of men out there who would love to be with me. *Plenty*." Sure, perhaps *love* was too strong of a word. But whatever. "I don't have to stand around and wait for someone who made it clear he can't trust me."

"Oh, I know there were plenty of others. First, I got the pic of you kissing that asshat Dylan."

Wait. What—he'd gotten a picture? Of her and Dylan? How? When?

Goosebumps rose on her arms. "That's how you knew about the kiss?" He hadn't mentioned a picture before. She'd walked into his home—*here*—and found him sitting on the couch with a bottle of beer gripped in his hands. When he'd looked up at her, rage had been burning in his dark eyes.

"*Second*...since you like to list things in order, I'll do it, too." His hands were loose at his sides, but his body was hard and tense. "*Second*...when I came to your station the next day to talk, I found the vase of roses on your desk. I'm a nosey SOB, so when I find out that someone sent *my* girlfriend roses, I pick up the card. Reflex action."

Those goosebumps got one hell of a lot worse. So bad that a whole shiver skated over her body because Rose remembered exactly what that card had said.

"*Thanks for an unforgettable night,*" War growled. "After reading that crap, I figured there was no point in talking. You had already moved the hell on to one of those guys who would *love* to be with you." His nostrils flared. "Funny thing, though. I don't see any of those dicks here now. I just see me. *I'm* the one who said he'd help you. I'm the one who—"

She felt a tear slip down her cheek.

War frowned at her. "Don't do that."

Rose swiped away the tear. "If I could make it stop, I would." She *hated* crying. But what he'd just said...

*Everything is worse.* This went much deeper than she'd thought. The killer had deliberately isolated her. Targeted her.

"That's another one," War noted, voice thickening. "Don't cry, dammit."

"If you don't like it, don't watch!" Another swipe over her cheek. "It's been one hell of a night, okay? It's probably adrenaline or after-effects or something. I'm not some super soldier. I'm not used to all of this like you are!"

"I was a SEAL, not a—"

"I didn't cheat on you." The words fell heavily into the room, and they were met by utter silence.

War's eyes glittered.

"I thought you knew me. That you would understand I could never do something like that to you." When she'd been with War, she had been hooked completely on him. Until they'd imploded. "Dylan kissed me when we were working late one night. I did *not* kiss him. As I said before, I immediately pushed him back. I was with you. I had no interest in him." *Or anyone else.* "I didn't know you had gotten a photo." She hadn't wanted to rehash all of this, but now it seemed necessary. "Do you know who sent the pic to you?"

His jaw was locked. He'd been jealous, possessive, when they were together. But they *weren't* together any longer. She was surprised he could still get riled up at this point. "War?" she prompted.

"No clue. I sent a text back but never got an answer. Figured it was just someone at the station who wanted me to know the score."

Someone had wanted him to know, all right.

"The night I came here..." Her gaze darted around. "The night you and I had that fight—had you just gotten the pic?"

"I got it a few hours before you arrived. It was a damn late night. You didn't get here until almost two a.m."

And that had made him think she was with Dylan during that time because she'd been so late for their date. Her eyes squeezed shut. "That's when it started. When I found the body and I tried to help. When I chased him..."

"Rose?"

Her eyes stayed closed. Maybe this way, she wouldn't cry. "I was terrified when I came here. I didn't know what to do. I knew I was in over my head. I'd talked to the cops, but I didn't think they believed what I was telling them. I came to you and—" And no point touching that. They both knew how the scene had ended. "Then the next day, he sent me the flowers." She'd been in his sights.

"Who did? Dylan?"

"No." Her eyes flew open. Another tear leaked down her cheek. "No, none of this is about him!" She jumped off the couch. Her body wanted to shake. "The killer, War. The killer sent the flowers. I think he sent you the picture of Dylan and me, too. I think he wanted me away from you." It was making sense now. So much sense.

*He studied me. Just as I was studying him.*

"Maybe he saw you as a threat. Maybe he thought—with your background—I would get you to help me. Or maybe he just didn't want to go up against you." She shoved back her hair. "Doesn't matter why, he just needed you out of the scene, so he removed you." By playing on War's jealousy. "He sent you the photo. You did the rest."

"Rose...I am not following."

Understandable. She was only just putting it all together herself.

War's fingers curled around her shoulders. A careful, gentle touch. He'd always been so careful when he touched her. "The beginning," he urged her. "Start there."

Her breath shuddered out. "I'd been covering the crime beat at the station." He hadn't been thrilled when she switched to that beat. He'd gotten extra growly and fierce. Rose knew he'd worried about her, so she hadn't told him a lot about her cases. She'd tried to protect him.

*Turned out, I was the one to need protection.*

Rose continued determinedly, "A woman reached out to me. She felt like someone was stalking her, but the police didn't have any evidence. It was like the man was a shadow, but she *felt* him. She wanted help, and I wanted to help her. I *tried* to help. But I couldn't find anything solid on him, either." Rose stopped.

War waited. His stare was so intense and deep, seeming to see right through her. "All of this was happening when we were together?"

"Yes."

"You didn't mention it to me."

"The night I was so late for our date, I got a frantic call from her. She needed me. By the time I got to her place, though..." She inhaled. "I found her on the floor of her bedroom. The sheet was still around her neck. I pulled it free. I tried to help her. I tried and—*I didn't know he was still there.*"

War's hold tightened on her. "What?"

"I didn't know he was watching me. Not until the next morning when I got the flowers from him with that stupid note. Like we'd shared something special together during the night."

War shook his head. "No."

"My DNA was all over her. I explained to the cops that I was there to help her. They told me to keep the story quiet because they were investigating. I did." She'd been too close to the case. To the victim. "I started digging, though. Realized there were other women in Florida who'd been strangled—two others within the last six months. A twenty-one-year-old had been strangled with a rope outside of Jacksonville. A thirty-three-year-old from Tampa had been found with a curtain wrapped around her neck. Then, here, in Pensacola, I found Janet Post." And that memory would always be burned in her mind. "Three days ago, he took another woman's life, Barbara Briggs. I tried to warn her. I desperately needed her to believe me about what was happening, but she didn't. Not until it was too late."

His hands were still curled over her shoulders. "How did you know he was going after her?"

She wasn't looking into his eyes. Her gaze had fallen to the strong column of his throat. But at War's question, her stare lifted to once again meet his. "Because he told me."

"What?"

"He's been contacting me. Ever since that night with Janet, he contacts me, at least twice a week. I was putting together everything he'd done, making a connection that the cops hadn't, and...I don't know if he liked the recognition or what, but he started calling me. He told me he would even give me a head start to save the next victim." This hurt so much. "He gave me stupid fucking clues, like we were playing a game together. Only it *wasn't* a game. It was real. It was someone's life. I was scared to death and desperate."

"*Rose...*" His shoulders shoved back in a hard roll. "The bastard has been *playing* with you?"

"I tried to save Barbara. I swear, I *tried*. I figured out the clues. I went to Barbara. I went to the cops. No one would listen. They thought I was just after a story. Then when Barbara died, and I'd been seen arguing with her, *after* I'd already been at the murder scene of another woman...guess who suddenly became such a major person of interest in the investigation?"

"If he was calling you, you have proof. You can give your phone records to the cops—"

"He used burner phones. I can't trace him. They can't trace him. All they have...is me."

"You can still talk to them—"

"My DNA was on Janet. I was seen arguing with Barbara. I was even in Tampa when the victim was killed there. A conference for reporters." She'd been *there.* "It looks bad. At the very least, the cops figure I might be involved with the killer."

"But you tried to save the victim."

"Tried and failed," she mumbled as she pulled away from him and paced toward the big picture window on the right. She heard the faint thunder of the waves as they crashed into the shore. "I'm not going back to the cops yet—you're giving me these forty-eight hours—because I'm still trying."

"I don't follow."

Squaring her shoulders, she turned back to War. "That's why I want forty-eight hours. I want a chance to stop him. If I'm on the loose, then he'll come for me." *Me, not anyone else.* "I think we proved that tonight." She swallowed the lump of worry in her throat. "If he stays focused on me, then no one else will get hurt. We can bring him down." She hoped. She held War's gaze. "There. That's the story. The big parts, anyway." She was so tired. "Let me sleep for...an hour. Two, max. Then we will find him." Then she'd stop feeling like she was breaking apart. "I can take the couch—"

"You'll take my bed."

Like she'd argue with taking that beautiful bed. Rose shuffled toward his bedroom.

But War stepped into her path. "But before you sleep, I have a few questions." There was something about his voice...that tone...

Her head tipped back.

"You really think he sent me the picture of you and Dylan?"

"Yes."

"Why?" A fast demand.

"Because I think I have been a target of his for a while. I think he wanted me isolated. He got me that way. He...watches his prey. Studies them. He studied me—and you. He figured out the way to break us apart."

His eyes narrowed. "The night I gave you hell...you'd just found a fucking body?"

She bit her lower lip. Managed a nod. "Janet's body."

His gaze shot away from her. *"Fuck me."* A ragged breath. "And you said the sonofabitch sent you those flowers that I saw on your desk?"

"I didn't know you'd seen them. I-I threw them away as soon as *I* saw them." War must have discovered the flowers before she had. She'd been late to work that day. "I found the delivery service that sent them, but they didn't know anything about him. He did the order online, and it turned out that he'd used a stolen credit card." It was an effort to stay upright. She felt so bone weary. "Any other questions?"

Silence. She took that as a no and started creeping for his bedroom again—

"One more."

Fine. If he was giving her his help, she'd answer the questions he had. Rose looked over her shoulder at him.

"Just how much do you hate me?"

Her heart slammed into her chest.

"Because it must be one hell of a lot. You were living in this nightmare, and you never came to me for help." His hands fisted at his sides. "So I ask again...just how much do you hate me?"

"I don't hate you." Soft. Tired.

"No?"

"You just hate me." With that, Rose entered his bedroom and quietly shut the door.

*** 

War's head fell forward. *You just hate me.* Rose's words replayed through his head. No, he didn't hate her. Never had.

But he'd sure as fuck screwed things to hell and back with her.

*All this time...all this freaking time...*

She'd been in danger, and he hadn't known. Some psycho out there had been terrorizing her, and he hadn't known. No clue at all. What if the SOB had killed her? What if War had just found her body?

His fists tightened.

When it came to Rose, he'd always been a jealous bastard. With everyone else, it had always been easy to keep his control in place. With her? He'd had to fight to contain his emotions.

She was so gorgeous to him. A walking wet dream. She could smile and make him go rock hard. But with her, it had been so much more than just a physical attraction. From the beginning, he'd known that he was sinking deep...

Then he'd begun to feel that she was pulling away. Lots of late nights...

Then the pic had come of Rose and Dylan.

*I wanted to pound my fist into that bastard's face.*

She'd shown up for their date hours later. From the moment she'd walked in, he'd known things were off with her. She hadn't looked him in the eye. Her movements had been slow. Nervous. He'd thought she was there to leave him.

*I was drunk so I said stupid shit.* He'd pushed her away. Pushed her away when she'd needed him.

*Fucking fuck!*

And too late...when War's head had cleared from the fog of rage and beer the next morning, he'd gone back to Rose so they could talk but...

*The fucking flowers.*

After reading the card, he'd left without seeing her. Pride was a bitch.

War had been set up. He got that. The prick out there had wanted him out of the picture.

*I'm back in the picture, asshole. And you will not get her.*

No matter what he had to do, War would make certain the killer hunting Rose was stopped.

\*\*\*

He slipped out of the bathroom with the towel knotted around his waist. He'd needed to get that stinking garbage smell off him, and War had crept inside the bedroom, then into the shower so he wouldn't wake Rose. As he made his way to the chest of drawers in his bedroom, his gaze darted to the bed. She was curled on her side, facing him, and one of her delicate hands was perched under her chin. Her features were soft, relaxed. Absolutely beautiful.

One long, sexy leg was kicked out from beneath the covers. She always slept that way. She'd told him once it helped to cool her down. He'd told her that seeing her leg had made him extra hot and—

*Get clothes. Get out.*

With silent steps, War stalked for his chest of drawers. He yanked out a pair of sweatpants. Since Rose was sleeping, he just let the towel fall before he yanked up the pants and—

"War." Soft. Husky.

He whirled around.

Her eyes were still closed. His breath whispered out. Time to go. Obviously, since he was starting to have damn auditory hallucinations about her calling his name. *Wishful thinking.* The couch was waiting. He took a step for the door.

"War?" More fretful. Worried.

Scared.

*Not* an auditory hallucination. Rose was calling for him. The hand that had been curled under her chin flew out and stretched in the air, as if she was searching for someone.

*For me.*

Slowly, he headed for the bed. He didn't want to wake her, but if she was having a bad dream—and after what she'd been through that night, a bad dream would be normal—he couldn't leave her that way. "It's okay," he heard himself rasp. "You're safe."

As she would always be, on his watch.

The furrow slid away from her forehead.

But for some reason, his treacherous fingers reached out and still smoothed that delicate area. A light caress over her—

She caught his wrist. Her eyes didn't open. "Stay?"

Such a bad idea. Bad for a thousand different reasons. And yet, when he opened his mouth, what he said was, "Yes."

# CHAPTER FOUR

"War?"

She turned toward him in bed and snuggled closer. Every muscle in War's body immediately tensed.

Her fingers trailed over his chest. A soft smile tugged at her lips, but her eyes didn't open. She'd been sleeping soundly, and this was not the wake up that he'd expected.

"You smell good," Rose murmured.

She smelled good enough to eat.

Her nose nuzzled against his throat. "Missed you," she told him, voice all husky and soft. Then she licked him. A quick, sensual little lick.

He was already rock hard. He'd been battling his arousal for her—hell, he didn't even know for how long. It was kind of just a perpetual state for him when Rose was near. But at that little lick, his body jolted. "Uh, Rose..." He should move. Get out of the bed. *Not* curl his arm around her and pull her even closer.

The woman was obviously still sleeping. She talked in her sleep sometimes. It was a cute trait. Except...

*She said she missed me.*

He cleared his throat. "Ah, Rose?" War tried again.

Her lips pressed to his throat.

His gaze snapped up to the ceiling. *You do not get to pounce on her. You do not get to—*

She suddenly stiffened. "What are you doing in my bed?" Rose demanded. No more soft and husky murmurs. The question was loud. Piercing. Probably designed to burst an ear drum.

She was apparently very awake right now.

Before he could respond, her head whipped up, and she narrowly avoided a sharp clip to his chin.

"War?" Her voice had gone up another octave.

"Technically..." He sat up. "It's my bed."

She sat up, too, and snatched the covers to her chest when she seemed to realize that she was only wearing a bra and panties. "You were supposed to take the couch!"

"I was going to do that. Absolutely. Very gentlemanly and all but then...you asked me to stay."

Her eyes could not possibly get any wider. "I did *not*."

"You did...*so*." He didn't pull the covers up. He had on his sweatpants, and they were stretched to the brink over a certain portion of his anatomy. The covers were currently pooled over that part of him, so he figured they could stay there instead of being needlessly yanked up to his chest.

Her gaze drifted down to his bare chest. She licked her lower lip. "I don't remember doing that."

"That's because you were dead to the world. But you were fretful and kinda sweet and when you asked me to stay, I decided...what would it hurt?"

She was still staring at his chest. "Did I do anything else?"

"Like what?" He liked the little flush in her cheeks.

"You know like what!"

"Well, you did lick me." His index finger slid over the side of his neck to show her the spot. Her gaze had lifted to follow his finger. "And I might have felt a little kiss."

At that revelation, her stare flew back to his. Her lips were parted, but she wasn't speaking.

"It's okay," he assured her. God, he wanted her mouth. "You still want me, and I—"

"I am not responsible for my actions when I am asleep! And you don't know what I want so do not presume to tell me."

"I will always want you," he finished. There. Done.

"Wh-what?"

"I said I will always want you. Just stating a fact. Thought you had realized it. Not like I can turn off the desire for you. It's just there."

She was still in the bed. So was he. He'd suspected she would jump up and run away at his confession.

She was holding her ground. "Why are you telling me this?"

"Figured you should know, since we'll be in close proximity for the next two days." Did he lean toward her a little bit? Yes, he did. His nostrils flared as he greedily inhaled her scent.

"What do you think is going to happen?" She seemed dazed. "That we are going to just return to the way things were? That I will just jump into bed with you?"

He looked at the bed. At her. *We kinda did jump into bed, sweetheart.*

"*War.*" Now she jumped *out* of the bed. Sadly. But she left the covers in her hurry and gave him a truly mind-blowing view of her body. "I was sleeping here. Not intending to seduce you. That was not part of my plan!"

Now he slowly rose from the bed. "Pity." It truly was. "It would be a master plan."

She blinked at him. "I do not get you." She stood on one side of the bed. He was on the other.

"For the record, I don't hate you, Rose. Hate is the last thing I feel." He stalked around the bed so that he could close in on her. She didn't back away. Her shoulders stiffened. Her chin notched up. But she didn't back up. If anything, she took a step...closer.

Her hair was tousled from sleep. She wore a sexy scrap of black lace for panties and a matching bra, and he was surprised he wasn't drooling as he stared at her.

"If you don't hate me, what do you feel?" Rose asked him.

His head began to lower toward her.

She crept closer to him. Her hands lifted as if she'd touch him. "What do you feel?" Rose breathed the words as she asked the question once more.

*I feel like I want to taste you. I want to devour you. I want—*

"War!" A bellow from the den. A familiar bellow that was immediately followed by the thud of heavy footsteps heading his way. "We need to talk, buddy, right the hell—"

The bedroom door flew open.

A tall, blond male with massive shoulders and a glower on his face stood in the doorway. As he took in the scene before him, his expression darkened even more. "Oh, no. *No.* Tell me you did *not* hook up with her."

War pushed Rose behind his body. "Get the hell out," War snapped to the blond.

He didn't get out. He kept glowering. "You didn't hook up with her. Did *not.* Not with Ms. Worst Mistake of My Life."

*Fucking hell.* "Odin, stop talking, now."

Normally, the guy *was* quiet. Why, oh, why did today have to be the one time his buddy got chatty?

"I warned you to keep your dick in your pants." And Odin was *still* talking. "Told you that she would mess you up again. But you swore you were done with her. Yesterday's news, I believe you said."

"*Stop. Talking.*"

"Yesterday's what?" Rose demanded from behind War.

Uh, oh. He'd worried that particular term would set her off. *Damage control time, stat.* War spun back toward her. "Sweetheart—"

She jabbed him in the chest with her index finger. "I am *never* yesterday's news. I am *breaking news*, you sonofabitch. I am the *lead story of the hour.* You want to make bullshit news jokes, then you at least get it right. *I am the feature news story of your life!"*

Odin coughed.

Without breaking eye contact with Rose—she was fucking glorious and sexy as hell—War ordered, "Odin, get the hell out of this room. Now."

But Odin lingered. "Thought you might want to know that as I was clearing out of the motel room, the cops were swarming. Someone must have tipped them off."

"The motel room?" Rose tried to jerk around War.

He wasn't in the mood to be jerked around, so he side-stepped with her. Mostly to make sure that she stayed covered from Odin's avid gaze. Odin didn't need to get a heavy visual of Rose's body and her lacy underwear.

"Found your handcuffs," Odin added. "And the blond wig. Guess all that featured heavily in the news story of the night?"

Oh, nice. Someone was trying to be funny. *He is your best friend. He is your best friend.* War mentally repeated the words twice. They didn't help cool him down. "Odin." Now, his voice was low and growling. Dangerous with intensity. "This is Rose." His gaze remained on her. "You will watch the fucking mouth with her. And you *will* give us privacy."

"Huh." A pause. "It's like that again?"

It was.

"Your funeral." The door closed a moment later.

Rose still glared up at War.

He could see that the 'yesterday's news' bit was gonna be a problem. "I can explain..."

"Do not. Don't even try. You're over me, and I'm over you."

It hadn't felt like they were over three minutes ago. It had felt like they were about to kiss. Like he was about to get his hands on her, get her hands on him, and that they would go supernova. "I—"

"You're in my rear-view mirror, too. Trust me. Like I said, I have no intention of picking up where we left off."

He was in her damn rear-view? Screw that. He curled his hands around her hips. Let his fingertips slide up over that silky skin of hers. He had missed touching her so much.

*I missed her.*

"What are you doing?" Nervous.

He was lowering his head toward her. He was thinking about taking her mouth with his and seeing if they would ignite the way they used to do. He was thinking about all the ways a man could be a fool.

"Don't kiss me," she whispered.

"Wasn't going to," he murmured right back.

He heard the hitch of her breathing. Saw the flare of her pupils even as she called, "Liar."

"I was going to wait for you to kiss *me*."

She shook her head. "Not happening."

"Then why are you staring so hard at my mouth?"

Immediately, her gaze whipped up to meet his.

He smiled. "Caught you."

"You're the one touching *me*."

"Because I like touching you. Like touching you. Holding you. Kissing you. Fucking you."

She swallowed.

"I don't think I'm in your rear-view, and I know you could *never* be yesterday's news."

Her tongue swiped over her lower lip.

His dick jerked. *Down, boy.*

"Then why did you say I was?" A hint of pain slid beneath her careful words.

"Because I'm a jackass." Truth. "Because men say stupid shit, especially when the woman of a guy's dreams walks out of his life."

"That's—I wasn't—"

His fingers slid away from her. "If you decide you want to kiss me, you know, just for the hell of it, don't worry. I'll be close by." He cocked his head to the left. "For the next two days, you'll know exactly where to find me. You say my name, and I'll be there."

"I need—"

*Yeah, baby. Tell me what you need. I will give it to you.*

"—to get dressed. So if you could just go hang out with your asshole friend, that would be great." She squinted. "Wait, how did he even get inside?"

"Odin has a key." A situation that would be changing.

"Why?"

"Because...I've been letting him crash here since he came to town." Odin had been having a hard time adjusting to civilian life. The beach had been a balm for War when he'd finished his service, and he'd hoped it would help to soothe his friend.

Except, some people couldn't be soothed. Not by anything or anyone.

Odin was definitely still a work in progress.

War's gaze drifted over Rose's body.

"Like what you see?" she fired at him.

"Fucking love it."

"*War.*"

"But then, you already know that." She was looking at his body, too, and there was no hiding his physical reaction to her. His dick was happily saluting in appreciation. "Get dressed. The last thing I want is for Odin to get hooked on you, too." Then he did a fast about-face and marched from the room.

He made sure to shut the bedroom door softly behind him.

War found Odin waiting for him. The man waited with his arms folded over his chest, and his legs leaning against the back of the couch.

"Were you drunk?" Odin asked.

"Church sober."

Odin's lips twisted. "I mean, I get the appeal. That body of hers will stop traffic, but—"

War strode straight for him. Stopped directly in front of Odin. "Forget what you saw."

"Excuse me?"

"Get amnesia. Don't think about her body or how fantastic it was. You don't need that memory. It's gone. Got me?"

Odin arched one eyebrow. "I think you have some serious issues where she is concerned. She *cheated* on you. She—"

"No. She didn't. Things are a hell of a lot more complex than I realized. She didn't cheat or lie. I'm an asshole. That's what you need to know for now."

A second eyebrow rose to join the first. "I don't need to know why you haven't turned her over to the cops? That was your plan, wasn't it?"

"The plan has been altered." There was more he wanted to say. Like how he already knew that the cops were searching the motel because he'd sent them there. But he didn't want Rose to hear that part, not yet. He needed to do some serious trust rebuilding with her before he revealed everything that was at play.

"Altered...because you slept with her?"

"Slept. That's all I did. No sex, but thanks for being all up in my business, buddy."

"I don't want you hurt again," Odin returned. "She *hurt* you. I've never seen you like that."

War fired a quick glance over his shoulder. The bedroom door was still closed. Satisfied, he focused on Odin once more. "Rose is in danger. The priority is to keep her safe and find the bastard who tried to kill her last night."

Shock flashed on Odin's face. "What?"

"He was strangling her," War confessed baldly. The memory had rage and fear blasting through him. "If I'd gotten in that motel room a little later, she would be gone."

All of the antagonism had fled from Odin's expression and body. "What can I do?"

And there it was. Pure Odin. The guy who would have your back in an instant even if he was pissed as hell at you. A friend straight to the core, through blood and pain and battles. Right now, *this* was their battle. Protecting Rose. Stopping the bastard after her. "You still have that tech guy who owes you some favors?" Odin had some pretty good tech skills himself, but he had an ex-spy buddy who was top-notch.

A quick nod.

"We're gonna need him."

The bedroom door opened. War exhaled and stepped to the side. Rose had dressed in jeans, a loose top, and sandals that showed off her cute feet with her blue toenail polish.

"Are you going to say rude things to me again?" Rose wanted to know as her gaze assessed Odin. "Because I am not in the mood for them."

Odin shook his head. "No more rude things from me."

Good. War pointed at Odin. "Play nicely while I get changed, and then we'll bring you up to speed."

"I'm always nice. Don't you remember? You're the asshole. I'm the charmer."

# CHAPTER FIVE

"I'm sorry."

Rose slanted a suspicious glance at the Thor look-alike. She'd been fiddling around in the kitchen, hunting for coffee, and he'd snuck up on her. For someone so big, he moved very quietly. Much like War. "For what?" she asked him. She'd slept far longer than she'd intended. By her calculations, she'd already lost at least four, maybe five, of her promised forty-eight hours.

"For the things I said. War set me straight. Told me you were innocent."

Innocent? Her brows rose as she turned fully toward him.

"I had...uh, heard you left him for someone else." A roll of one massive shoulder. "He just said that wasn't the case. So, yeah..." Halting. Rough. "I shouldn't have been a dick. I was trying to protect my friend, and I overstepped."

"You *were* a dick." She wouldn't let that pass. "War is also the one who broke up with *me*. If you want to give someone a hard time, maybe you can try giving him a bit of hell, hmm?"

"Duly noted." His blue eyes seemed to gleam. Like he found her response funny. She wasn't being funny.

"Great," Rose muttered. "Glad we cleared that up. Now...what is there to eat in this place? I am starving." She yanked open the refrigerator. Rummaged around and found some grapes. They looked mostly fresh, so she popped a few in her mouth. When she looked up, she found the blond had ambled closer. "What?"

"I'm Odin."

"I thought you were Thor...?"

His eyebrows wrinkled.

She ate a few more grapes. "But, sure, Odin works, too. I can see it." She grabbed some orange juice. Maybe the Vitamin C would pep her up. "I'm Rose. Though you already knew that."

He inclined his head.

She drank the orange juice. He didn't say more.

Just stared at her.

So...*this isn't fun.* Slowly, she put down her empty glass. Her fingers tapped on the counter as she stared at him. "You've been crashing here, hmm?"

A nod.

"Where were you before you crashed?"

"Finishing my duty."

"Ah. Another SEAL?" The guy had military written all over him. That short blond, no-nonsense cut. The way he held his body so alertly. The strength that she could see clinging to him—

"Delta Force."

It was like pulling teeth to get responses. "You were way chattier in the bedroom."

"That's because I thought my best friend had just committed a colossal mistake. I was worried."

She stopped tapping her fingers and strolled toward him. "You were wrong."

"I already admitted that. I said—"

"I meant when you called yourself a charmer. I don't know who told you that lie, but it was mean. You should know, you have not been very charming so far in our relationship."

One eyebrow crooked up. "No? I'll try to work on that."

The bedroom door opened. "You two getting along?"

"Fabulously," Rose assured him. Her gaze automatically darted toward War. He'd tugged on a white t-shirt and jeans. Battered boots. His hair was shoved back. He looked tough, dangerous, and sexy. Three things that tended to turn her on way too much.

*Yesterday's news.*

That insult slithered through her mind and made her spine stiffen. She'd show him yesterday's news. She had a new mission, and it was to make War beg before their forty-eight hours were done. In fact, she'd see just how fast she could get him eating out of her hand—

"Need these?" Odin lifted a pair of handcuffs.

She slanted him an unamused glance. "*Not* charming."

"No?"

War took the cuffs.

"Why the hell are you getting those?" Suspicion knifed through her. "You promised me that you'd give me forty-eight hours. There is no way you are cuffing me again."

"Relax."

Telling a person to *relax* never made anyone actually relax. How did War not know that?

"I don't know what we might find on our hunt. I have to be prepared. I'm taking the cuffs. I've got my knife strapped inside my boot. And I'll make sure that my gun is with us, too." He closed in on her. "The cuffs are for the bastard we're after, but, if you try to leave me, if you try to run away on your own, I will cuff you to me."

"Threats aren't the way to make friends," Rose chided him even as nerves had her stomach fluttering. He looked all mad, bad, dangerous...and sexy.

"I'm not interested in being your friend."

Her gaze cut away from him. Mostly because his words had hurt. For a while there, she *had* thought they were friends. Friends. Lovers.

*Back to the plan of having him beg...*

"Rose?" His hand lifted toward her.

She stepped back. "I know where our first stop should be."

"By all means, do share that info."

"Billy was a no-show at the restaurant last night. He, ah, he was supposed to help me find a new safe house for crashing."

"And this Billy is...?" War prompted.

"Someone I trust. Billy has lots of connections in this area. He's helped me. I've helped him."

"He's an informant for her," Odin supplied.

"He's a *friend,*" Rose corrected. "A friend who passes on information when he has it. He's an information trader, and he should have been there last night. Billy has never let me down before, and I-I have to check on him. After I left you at the restaurant, I darted by his place, but he wasn't there. I'm hoping he's back by now. We *need* to check on him."

"Damn straight, we do." War's voice was curt. "Because you might consider him a *friend,* but from where I stand, the guy could have set you up."

She started to shake her head.

"Maybe he sold *you* out, Rose. Gave the perp after you a tip that you'd be at the restaurant. Then the freak followed you back to your motel. Only I was there, too. The perp waited until I slipped out, and he attacked."

A lump lodged in her throat. She choked it down. "Billy wouldn't do that to me."

War didn't look convinced. "Does this Billy happen to have a record? Any run-ins with the law?"

Her lips pressed together.

"Right. Yeah. That's what I thought. Let's definitely go make a stop by his place." He caught her hand in his. "Time to get the show rolling."

His touch sent a jolt through her, and she gave a little jerk in helpless response.

His knowing gaze said he'd caught the movement.

"Want me on your six?" Odin asked in his deep, rumbling voice.

"What is that?" Though Rose had a pretty good idea, she still wanted to be certain. "That mean you're gonna be tailing us and watching War's back?"

"I want *you* talking to your tech buddy." War reached into his pocket and tossed a phone at

Odin. Odin caught it with one hand. "Rose has been getting calls from the SOB, and I think I got a text from him a month ago. That's my phone—the one he contacted me on. See if you can track him down."

"On it."

"You know I have a second phone. The one I use when working certain cases—if you need me, call me on that line."

A quick inclination of Odin's head. "What else can I do?"

"You said the cops were at the motel. If they find anything useful, I want to know about it."

"Done."

"Thanks, man. I owe you."

Her gaze darted between the two men.

Odin shook his head. "No, you don't owe me." A muscle flexed along his stubble-covered jaw. "The way I figure it, we won't be even until I save your life. Payback for you dragging me and my bloody body over two miles until you could get me help."

"I didn't *drag* your sorry ass. I carried you. There's a difference." A half-smile lifted War's lips, only to vanish in a blink. "He could be close. Make sure you don't lower your guard."

Odin's stare shifted to her. "And you'll have her?"

"Yes. I will have her." When War's gaze turned to Rose, it was hot. Determined. Possessive. "Count on it."

\*\*\*

"You don't *have* me," Rose announced as they made their way to War's waiting vehicle. The waves slammed into the shore. "That was some weird alpha BS that just will not play with me—"

He angled toward her. "I meant that I was seeing to your protection. You won't be hurt while I'm here."

"Then...you could have just said that."

It *was* what he'd said. "Odin understood." Though War most certainly would like to *have* her, too. That was on the agenda. Having her in any and every way imaginable.

Without another word, she climbed into his vehicle. He slid in after her. Started the car. Had them on the road in moments. She rattled off directions, and he nodded because he knew the area she was talking about.

"I'm sorry...for the scene with Odin." The words felt rusty. He wasn't used to apologizing. "He was trying to look after me. Odin thinks he owes me."

"I got that part." He could feel her gaze on him. "Did you really carry him two miles?"

"No."

"Oh, he seemed—"

"It was six, but I would have carried him sixty if it meant I could get him help. Odin and I go back a long way."

"You...never mentioned him to me before."

He turned right. Glanced in the rear-view mirror. Dawn hadn't come yet, and no headlights showed in the darkness behind him. War wanted to make sure they weren't being tailed. He was not in the mood for surprises. "Before, whenever I was with you, I was ripping off your clothes. Making you scream with pleasure. Driving us both crazy. There weren't always lots of moments for *talking*."

"You wouldn't let me get close."

Now he laughed. "Baby, you were plenty—"

"Physically close is one thing. I always felt like you were blocking me off from anything else."

Trust wasn't easy for him. Never had been. And someone had used that against them both. *You will pay.* "I never knew my mom. She skipped out after I was born. My dad stayed around a few more years before he vanished, too. Odin's family...they are the ones who raised me." Did she get what he was doing? He was *trying* to share with her. "I didn't have the picket fence and the perfect home like you did. I liked hearing more about you and your life than telling you the mess that mine had been." He risked a glance her way.

Her head was turned toward him.

"But then you started to pull away. At the end, you were keeping secrets, and I could tell. That last night, you didn't show for our date...you didn't call for hours. I just had that fucking photograph to drive me crazy." *To make me wild with jealousy because you were mine.* "I didn't know...what was happening. *You* didn't let me in." *If I'd known you were in danger, nothing would have pulled me away. Nothing.* He cleared his throat. "How about for the rest of our time together, you don't hold info back from me. You tell me exactly what is happening. If you don't..." Because he was worried she still had secrets. Secrets that might get her killed. "I will break our deal and hand you over to the cops," he finished grimly.

"What? No, War, you promised—"

"Don't hold out on me, and we won't have a problem." Simple enough.

"I am *not* holding back."

"No?"

"No."

"Good." He wanted to believe her, he really did but...

When he risked another glance at her, she'd turned away. Whenever Rose lied, she always turned away.

# CHAPTER SIX

"You sure this is the spot?" War eyed the dark house before him. "It looks like no one has been here in months."

"Appearances are deceiving. Billy lives here. He likes to stay off the radar, and he's not exactly big on landscape work. So the yard is overgrown." Overgrown was an exceedingly kind understatement. The grass was about two feet high, and the springing branches from the bushes covered the house's front windows. Her previous check by the house had been fruitless. Rose was hoping Billy had returned home now. She wet her lips. "What's the plan? Are we going to knock on the front door? Are we going to sneak in the back? Are we—"

"We're going to grab the asshole who is running for the motorcycle right now."

Wait—what? They were going to—

Before she could question him, War had jumped out of the car. She scrambled after him. She hadn't even seen the motorcycle until that moment—it was camouflaged by the bushes, too. And, sure enough, there was a hooded figure hurrying toward the bike.

"Billy!" she called.

He whirled toward her, and he brought up a knife.

She froze.

War didn't. He jumped in front of her. "Put the knife down, *now*."

"Who the hell are you?" Billy's voice shook. Billy was around twenty-two. Muscled, but nowhere near War's size.

"I'm the man who is giving you three seconds to put down the knife before I lose my patience and I take it from you." He took a step forward. "One."

"Billy, it's me! Drop the knife!" Rose urged him.

"Two."

*Gah!* This was not the way to calm down a tense situation. "War, your counting is *not* helping!"

Billy's hand was shaking, but he hadn't dropped the knife. She couldn't let this scene get worse. "He's with me, Billy. He's not a threat!"

"Looks like a threat," Billy muttered.

Okay, fine, granted, War looked like a threat on most days, but—

"Three." War ripped the knife from Billy's hand. Like it was nothing. Then he threw the knife toward the bushes and slammed Billy back against the side of the house. "I don't think I like you, Billy."

She crowded closer to them. "Billy, why did you come at us with a knife?"

"Just saw him at first...not you. When some big bastard comes at me, I need to defend myself!"

War easily held him pinned. She didn't point out that Billy didn't appear to be doing a very good job of defending himself in that moment. Her gaze raked over him. "You don't look injured," she noted. That was a good thing, of course. She was glad he was okay, but unease still slithered through her. "I was worried something had happened to you when you didn't make our meeting at Finch's."

"Yeah...about that..." He strained against War.

War shoved him back with what appeared to be no effort.

"Something came up, all right?" Billy snarled. "Couldn't make it. No big deal."

"It's a very big deal," War assured him. "So big that it makes me want to kick your ass."

"War." Her hand closed around his shoulder. "Let him go."

Growling, he dropped his hands, but War didn't back up far. "Come at me with a knife again," he warned Billy, "and I will break your hand."

"Jesus!" Billy gaped at War, then at her. "Where did you find him? And can you send him back? Because he's scary and psychotic!"

"What came up, Billy?" Rose asked. Dawn was finally starting to streak across the sky. Angry red streaks.

"I...you know. Stuff." A rough shrug.

No, she didn't know and that was why she'd asked. "You said you'd have a place for me to stay."

"You can stay here." He jerked a thumb over his shoulder toward his house. "I'm cutting out of town for a few days. Feel free to crash here while I'm gone."

He was leaving town. Running. He hadn't met her at Finch's. She could connect the dots. "You sold me out?"

"I just...I mean...hell, it's not a big deal. Don't make it a deal." His voice cracked. "Some guy called and offered me a grand if I could set up a meeting with you. Some fool with a crush. Said he saw you on TV and wanted to meet you."

She shook her head. He couldn't be serious.

"Thought he was joking, then I found five hundred bucks on my doorstep. I gave him the address of the restaurant last night, and then I got five hundred more dollars a bit later. Easy money, you know?"

War grabbed him and slammed Billy back against the house once more.

"Not again!" Billy snapped. "Would you stop doing this shit?"

"*He tried to fucking kill her.*" War's voice was ice cold. "You set her up to die."

"What? No, *no!*" Billy heaved. War didn't let him go. "Rose, it was just a fan! I gave him the address for Finch's. It was no big deal!"

"It was a very big deal." The unease in her stomach had turned into thick knots. "And you're lying right now. You knew the cops were looking for me. You knew I was hiding. But you still want me to believe you just gave me up to some stranger for money? That you believed he had a crush on me?" No, not happening. "What really went down?"

"I *told* you—"

"I have my own knife," War said. "Want to see what I can do with it?"

"No! No, no, Rose, call him off!"

"He's not an attack dog. The man doesn't do what I say. If he wants to show you what he can do with his knife..." She forced a careless tone as if it didn't matter to her. "Then I guess we are all about to see what he can do with his—"

"He attacked me, all right? Some jerk broke into my house while I was sleeping. When I woke up, he had a freaking rope around my throat. Said if I didn't tell him where to find you, I was dead."

Now those words held the desperate ring of truth. "Why didn't you go to the cops?"

"Because I already have two warrants out for my arrest! I go to them, and they'll toss me in a cell. I figured the best thing for me was to just get my ass out of town."

"*After* you sold her out," War said in disgust. "You didn't care if Rose got hurt, as long as your own ass was safe."

"It wasn't *personal*. But he was gonna kill me! What was I supposed to do?"

"I thought we were friends," Rose whispered. "You could have at least called and told me he was going to be there. Given me a head's up—"

"He said if you weren't there, he'd come back for me. That's why I'm running. It's been fun working with you, but nothing is worth my life. I'm getting the hell out of here, and, seriously, you should do the same. Ditch this town. Look for greener pastures and all that."

"*What did he look like?*" War's voice was still flat. Still cold enough to send goose bumps running down her body.

"I don't know! He was big. It was dark. I was trying to stay *alive*. His voice was low, whispery. That's all I got."

Nothing they could use to identify the guy. Just like her own attack. She'd only been aware that he was big. His mask had completely hidden his face. He hadn't talked to her when he'd attacked. She and War had heard his drawling voice when he'd been calling to her from *outside* of the motel room, but she suspected he might have been faking the heavy accent he'd used.

"I don't know anything else, I swear."

She could hear the fear in Billy's words. It seemed genuine. "War, we need to leave."

War slowly released Billy.

"Thought he didn't do what you said," Billy mumbled.

Her hands slid down War's arm as she kept her focus on Billy. "I came by because I wanted to make sure you were okay. I was worried about you."

His head ducked toward his chest. "Look, I told you, it wasn't personal. But the man was gonna kill—"

"You have to watch out for yourself. I got it. Understood. Take care, Billy. I never meant for you to get pulled into this mess." The last thing she wanted was for someone else to get hurt. She tugged on War's arm. "Let's go."

But he was an immovable object.

She tugged again. "War?"

His gaze was on Billy. "She's not alone."

"Uh, what?"

"You're watching out for yourself, and I'm watching out for her. Pass the word. Rose isn't on her own. If that freak comes to get her, he'll find me waiting. And if you *ever* put her in jeopardy again, you'll see just what I can do with my knife. That's a promise." War stared at Billy until he seemed satisfied that his words had made their impact. Only then did he step back.

Billy weaved.

War took her hand in his. Led her toward the Impala. He settled her in the passenger seat. Slammed her door. Then stalked around the car to the driver's side.

She watched him in silence. There was a hard, dangerous tension riding him. War pulled out his phone—and since when did he have *two* phones? She didn't remember that from their time together, but when she'd asked him about the second phone earlier, he'd told her it was for PI business. He hadn't shared more. Now, he put the phone to his ear and curtly said, "The jackass wants to flee town," and he rattled off Billy's address.

"Are you talking to Odin?" Must be. His partner in crime.

War grunted. "Take care of it." He ended the call. Got them away from the scene with a squeal of his tires.

Rose didn't speak, not until they were well away from Billy's place... "You can be scary."

His hold tightened around the wheel. "You never had a need to see that side of me before."

No, she didn't guess that she had. "Have you...have you ever killed anyone?"

"Don't ask questions that you don't want answered."

She'd take that as a yes. She'd seen the scars on his body. One that she knew was from a bullet wound. Another long slash across his abdomen that must have come from a knife. "I don't want you to kill for me."

His jaw hardened. "That guy is not your friend."

"Billy was scared. He thought he would die. When people are scared, they do desperate things."

"He traded your life for his without a second's hesitation. I wouldn't do that. *Know* it."

She...did. "What am I going to owe you for this?"

He fired a fast glance her way. "What are you talking about?"

"The price for the forty-eight hours. When this is over, what will I have to pay you?" He'd said Dylan was paying him twenty grand. She didn't have that kind of cash lying around. Maybe War would let her do some sort of payment plan?

"We'll cross that bridge when the time comes. Right now, we have other issues."

"Right." They had lots of issues. "Like finding the killer. Getting good evidence to lock him away. Like—"

"Like the asshole who has been tailing us ever since we left Billy's."

She started to whip her head around—

"*Don't*. Don't look back. We want him to think he's catching us off guard."

Her heart thundered in her chest. He *had* caught her off guard. She'd been way too distracted when they left Billy's.

"I've got a plan."

"Wonderful to know." Her gaze cut to the passenger side mirror.

"If he wants to follow us, then we'll lead him into a trap."

Seriously?

"My bar is empty right now. We're taking him there."

And it wasn't too far away. Yes, okay, but... "Don't you dare get hurt." An order that blurted from her.

He gave a low, rumbling laugh. "Don't worry. I'll be the one doing the hurting."

\*\*\*

The bar hadn't changed much. Granted, it had only been a little over a month since she'd last stepped inside Armageddon, so it wasn't as if Rose had expected something major. Nestled in the entertainment district of downtown Pensacola, Florida, the bar had become a hotspot shortly after opening. Rough, dark, and with the best whiskey in town, people had flocked to get inside.

But one memorable night, only she and War had been there. He'd shut the bar down for them.

Lifted her up on that long, gleaming, wooden counter. Shoved her skirt up high—

"We need to move, Rose. I left the door open so he'd have easy access."

Her gaze jerked away from the counter. "You left it open? Was that a good idea?" It sounded like a terrible idea to her. Worst. Ever.

His fingers curled around her wrist, and he eased her toward a small hallway. He pulled her into the hallway just as she heard the squeak of the front door's hinges.

War had her caged with his body. His hand lifted, and he put his index finger to his lips.

Her head moved in a quick, jerky nod. Her heartbeat echoed in her ears, and she found that she could not look away from his dark gaze.

But over the thunder of her heart, she heard...footsteps. Slow. Uncertain.

The guy had taken the bait. Whoever their tail was, the man had followed them inside of Armageddon.

War slid his hand behind his back. Then he pulled out a gun. He'd taken that gun out of his glove box and tucked it behind his shirt before they'd gone into the bar. "*Stay. Here.*" He mouthed the words.

She'd thought the plan was for them to stick together. She didn't remember any version of this situation where he was supposed to leave her and go without—

He was already gone.

Rose flattened her body against the wall. She barely breathed as she waited to see—or rather, hear—what would happen next. And then...

*"Don't take another step."* War's cold command. Loud. Clear.

Then, equally loud...but terrified, *"This is a mistake! A big mistake!"*

"Absolutely," War agreed. "And you're the one who made it. You never should have walked into my bar, and you damn well should have never hurt *her.*"

# CHAPTER SEVEN

The man standing in front of War cried out, "I haven't hurt anyone!" His hands were up, palms out, and his wide, watery eyes were terrified. "Look, please, let me just show you my ID..." His right hand began to lower.

"Don't." War shook his head. "You do not want to be reaching for something right now. Not when you just followed me across town. Not when you just broke into my bar—"

"The door was open!"

"And not after you tried to kill *my* girl last night—"

A gulp. His Adam's apple bobbed. "I did not try to kill anyone! Look, I'm a PI! Just like you."

War's gaze swept over the guy's khaki pants and tweed coat. Tweed? Who the fuck wore tweed? "You are nothing like me."

"Dylan hired me, too! He was afraid you wouldn't report to him, so I was supposed to tail you. I swear, I haven't hurt anyone, now put the gun down!"

"Yeah, you're not giving orders. You're going to keep your hands up. I'm going to come to you, I'll reach inside your ever-so-interesting coat pocket, and I'll check your ID. Then we'll see where we go from that point."

A quick nod. The man with the dark red hair kept his hands up.

Taking his time, War crossed to him. He reached inside the coat pocket. Pulled out the wallet. Studied the driver's license. And the PI license. "Gary Strom. I've heard about you." The name was familiar. The face had been, too. But War had still wanted to see the ID. "Don't you usually spend your hours taking photos of cheating spouses?"

Gary sniffed. "I help people who have been betrayed. There is *nothing* wrong with that sort of work."

He put the ID back in the wallet and shoved it into Gary's coat pocket. "And now you are tailing me."

"I'm looking for *her*."

"Her?" He let his brows climb as he stepped back.

"I saw you come in with her. You have Rose."

War glanced around the bar. "Do you see her? Because I don't."

"I know she's here. Just so you're aware, before I even came inside, I texted Dylan to let him know, too. I was not about to be cut out of my 1k."

"A thousand? That's what he's paying you to tail me?"

"He didn't think you'd turn her over like you said. Guy is worried about his station's reputation. Said she'd seduce you and get you to help her."

"She could certainly try," War allowed. *I would love to see that.* "*If* she was here, the woman would be welcome to seduce me all she liked." He was sure Rose would hear those words.

"Look, I—"

"Get the hell out of my bar, Gary."

Gary spun and ran. War followed him, a lot more slowly, and he turned and flipped the lock at the door once Gary was gone. Consideringly, he tilted his head and ran through possibilities.

"If that guy contacted Dylan, he'll be showing up here soon."

War stiffened at the sound of Rose's voice. Then he slowly turned to face her.

She stood near the bar. One hand slid nervously along the edge of the wood. He stalked toward her. Put the gun on a nearby table. Finished closing in on her.

"War?"

"If he's coming, we should make sure we give Dylan a good show."

"I don't understand."

He was right in front of her. War stared down into Rose's eyes. "Are you going to seduce me? Good old Gary thought that might be on your agenda."

"I..." She shook her head. "What is happening right now?"

He slid his hand under the curtain of her hair. "Wouldn't be hard. Like I told you before, when you're near, I get hard. Wanting you is second nature to me."

She sucked in a sharp breath. "Why are you saying these things?"

"Because I'm supposed to be working for your asshole producer. But instead, I'm hiding you. He knew that was what I would do. So he sent in a backup to watch me and report on what he saw. Dylan probably thought I planned to screw him over all along. Take the twenty grand and take *you*." Ever so tempting. Actually, it was one of the best plans he'd heard in ages. "Since Dylan knows I can't stand him, it was probably a good idea for him to get a backup PI."

Her hands rose. Fluttered in the air. Hesitated, as if she wanted to touch him.

"I don't fucking trust Dylan," he growled.

"Yes, yes, I know and—"

"The guy who just left? Gary Strom is a PI who makes his living hiding in bushes and taking sleazy pictures of people in compromising situations."

He saw her eyes widen.

"Exactly," War murmured. "Just like the compromising picture I got of you. The picture that was a setup. Now we know that Dylan has a working relationship with Gary, and that makes me very, very suspicious."

"Suspicious? Wait...you think Dylan—"

"You said you were at a conference in Tampa when one of the murders occurred?"

A cautious nod.

His hand was still in her silken hair. "Was Dylan there, too?"

He saw the answer on her face before she even said a word. His gut clenched.

"Yes. But, War, look, Dylan is a jerk, yes, but he's not a killer."

War wasn't so sure. "We're going to find out."

"Not like he's just going to confess if he is guilty!"

"No, not right away, he won't. That's why we find evidence. That's what you hired me for, remember?"

"I...we haven't even talked about what I'll owe you."

"No?" His eyebrows climbed. "Thought we did. Thought we covered that you were seducing me into helping you."

Her cheeks flushed. "That's not what I was doing!"

His head lowered toward her. "But that's what we'll want Dylan to believe. Dylan and anyone else who may be watching when we leave in the next few minutes. Sell that story. Get used to having me touch you again. Get used to my hands and my mouth. Because when we walk out that door, we are going to put on a show." He'd lay odds that Gary was out there with his camera at the ready.

*You are gonna report back to Dylan, aren't you? Then let's give you something good to report.*

"Do you think we should practice, just to make sure we can still get it right?" His gaze was on her mouth. He loved her mouth. Plump lips. Sexy and soft.

"No." A faint exhale from her. "We...no. I don't need to practice."

He wanted her mouth. He *would* have it. But his hand slid away, and he backed up. "Then I'll trust you to smile for the camera and put on a killer performance when we step outside."

She hesitated. "War, is this necessary?"

"Yes." That was all he'd say. *Very, very necessary.*

Just as coming to the bar had been necessary. He had the place wired for security. Most folks never noticed the little cameras that he had at the doors. He didn't think dumbass Gary had noticed. But now War had video footage of the guy tailing him. Proof, for later.

If Dylan was on his way to the bar, then this was the perfect time to check out that jerk's place. *While it's nice and empty.* "Let's do this." He slid his arm around her shoulder, tucked her against him, and got ready for his close-up.

When he threw open the bar's front door, the street outside appeared empty. Only his car waited near the curb. No sign of Gary, though he was sure the other PI was close by. War walked Rose to the car, but he didn't open her door. Instead, he pulled her against him.

Then he took her mouth.

He was setting up the shot. Just as he now suspected Dylan had done. A shot of a couple kissing. The shot that had sent jealousy burning through War's mind and body and had shattered his control. The shot that had—

"War," Rose breathed against his mouth, and he forgot everything else.

A savage growl broke from him as his hands tightened around her hips. He pulled her tighter against him as his mouth opened wide on hers. His tongue thrust into her mouth. Tasted her. Fuck, she was good. Delicious. Her tongue met his as she pressed close to him. Her could feel her breasts pushing at him, her tight nipples. He wanted her nipples in his mouth. Wanted his dick in her. Wanted her screaming his name and squeezing him with her sex as her orgasm poured through her and he slammed deep looking for his own release. He wanted—

His hands were sliding under her shirt. He was touching warm, smooth skin.

*Stop. You've got an audience.* That had been the plan, originally. To put on a show. But he didn't intend to fuck Rose in front of anyone. When they were together, that time was *theirs*. No one else would see her that way. His head lifted. His breath panted out even as his cock shoved hard against the front of his jeans.

Rose's lips were red and swollen from his mouth. Her thick lashes slowly lifted even as her tongue slid over her lower lip, as if catching the last bit of his taste.

His body tensed even more.

"Was that...good enough?" she asked softly.

It was freaking perfect in his book. Just as hot and sensual as always.

"Did we give him a good picture?"

A picture? Oh, yeah. Right. Shit. A picture. His eyes narrowed. Desire had him on the edge, but Rose was whispering to him like she'd just been faking her hungry reaction to him. His head started to lower. He'd kiss her again and see—

"It's not safe to just stay out here like this. Someone might recognize me."

He yanked open her door. She quickly slid inside. Looked up at him. "War? Are you all right?"

Oh, he just had a severe case of blue balls, but that was his own damn fault. He wanted to fuck her more than he wanted to breathe but again...his fault. He slammed the door shut and hurried for his side of the vehicle.

Gary ducked behind a nearby building. "Go screw yourself, Gary," War called. At least the other PI had gotten the shots. Dylan would be seeing them soon.

Good.

War revved the engine. His baby rolled away like the boss she was.

Her voice husky, a little breathless, Rose admitted, "I don't—I don't get why that was necessary."

Ah, back to that, were they? He didn't respond right away. Instead, he focused on breathing and trying not to notice the mouth-watering way she smelled.

"War? Why is it so important for Dylan to see us together?"

"Because I want him to know you're off-limits." *Because he tried to take you away, and I still need to make him pay for that.* "I don't trust him, Rose. The fact that he's been pulling all the strings behind the scenes makes me suspicious as hell. *That's* why we're going to his place right now. I want a look inside. He'll be busy rushing to meet Gary, and it will give us the time we need."

"Wait. Back up. You're seriously talking about searching his place. My producer's home."

That was exactly what he was talking about. War checked his rear-view. No sign of Gary.

"You don't actually think that Dylan could be the killer, do you? I mean, it's Dylan. Pompous, annoying, but hardly serial killer material."

"Sometimes, you don't know a person as well as you think." He cut her a glance. "Everyone has secrets."

She tucked a lock of hair behind her ear.

"He hired me to find you. He hired Gary. And as soon as I made contact with you, the masked killer attacked."

Her face did an adorable scrunch as she thought. "The attacker didn't say a word when he fought with me in that bathroom."

His gaze slid back to the road. "Maybe he didn't speak because he was afraid you'd recognize his voice. Ten to one odds say he was faking that accent when he pretended to be the Good Samaritan."

"I've already suspected the same thing about the accent. That it was fake."

"When you're fighting with someone, when you're trying to kill someone, your control isn't the best. Maybe it was too hard to fake an accent then, so he just stayed quiet and focused on the job."

"The job," she repeated. "Killing me?"

"It's *not* going to happen. Told you that already. He will not put his hands on you again." That was a promise. A War Channing guarantee.

# CHAPTER EIGHT

The kiss had caught her off guard. She had thought that her response to War would be different. Rose certainly hadn't expected to feel the brush of his mouth against hers and then have her control ripped away.

But that was precisely what had happened.

She'd been rubbing her body against his, arching into him, opening her mouth wider, tasting him, licking him—and wanting so much more. Her nipples had gone tight. Her panties had gotten wet and all along, it had just been pretend. For him, anyway.

He'd been putting on a show. Delivering a screw-you message to Dylan.

While she'd been falling back into a dangerous habit. Wanting War? Yes, that was very, very dangerous.

"We're turning here." His words whispered into her ear.

It hadn't taken long to get to Dylan's place. He owned one of the historic homes about five minutes away from Downtown Pensacola. A two-story house with a wrap-around porch and views of the bay, the place was gorgeous. He often threw parties for the station employees at his home, so she'd been there a few times. She certainly hadn't ever seen anything suspicious while she'd been inside. Maybe she'd seen some bad, overpriced decorating, but that had been it.

"He has a camera at the front door, so we're going in the back," War told her. He'd parked the car a good distance away from Dylan's home, and he'd just gotten off the phone on another one of his quick, mysterious calls. "I'll handle disabling the security."

"How are you going to handle that, exactly?"

He flashed her his half-grin as he slid from the car. "Trust me, I got it."

She *was* having to trust him. Completely. With her life. War held her future in the palms of his strong hands and the very fact that they were about to pull a B&E on her *producer*...

She shoved open her door and hurried toward War. "Anything we find here won't be admissible. We can't just break into someone's house and steal evidence." The street was deserted. A good thing.

"Relax."

Utterly impossible in that moment.

"I'm not planning to steal anything. Try having some faith, would you?"

*You could do the same.* She bit back the retort. Now wasn't the time to rehash their past.

"Put these on." He handed her a pair of gloves. Slid on a pair himself.

Someone had sure come prepared. "Why are you so well supplied? Been committing crimes often lately?"

"Wouldn't you like to know?"

Yes, she would. That was why she'd asked.

War took her gloved hand, and they quickly slipped to the back of the house. He was doing such a good job of keeping them concealed as they moved that if she hadn't known better, Rose would have thought he'd broken into Dylan's place before.

*Um, I don't know better.* Because he went right for the hidden key in the back. A key that she hadn't realized was there. He took it from one of those places cut into the underside of a fake rock, and then he made his way for the door.

Once they were inside, War beelined for the security keypad. A few quick taps, and the alarm was disengaged.

"How did you do that?" Suspicion had Rose squinting at him. She kept her voice low. Hushed.

"I'm a PI, Rose. If I can't get past a basic security setup, it would be embarrassing."

"But you didn't even try multiple codes. You got it right on the first attempt," she whispered. They were in Dylan's kitchen, one filled with gleaming granite countertops and white cabinets, and nerves had her fingers fluttering as she spoke.

"You brought me to a party here once, remember? I saw him put in the code back then. Someone broke a window and the alarm sounded so he had to punch in the info. I remembered the code from that time."

"Oh." That made sense. The breaking glass had triggered a shrill alarm. "For a minute there," she tip-toed up behind him, "I thought maybe you'd broken in before."

"It's *not* my first B&E," he breathed back as his head turned and his mouth brushed along the shell of her ear. "And it's not yours, either."

A shiver slid over her because she was sure she'd felt the lick of his tongue against her. He was also right. This wasn't her first time to sneak into a place that didn't belong to her. Though the circumstances for the other had been different.

Not like she was some kind of career criminal or anything.

"You don't have to keep whispering. He doesn't have cameras or audio recorders in the house."

"How do you know?" She was peering into all of the corners.

"Because I got a thorough tour of the place during that previous visit. Now, come on, we don't have a lot of time."

They got to work. Rose wasn't one hundred percent sure what she was even looking for—a picture, a note, something that would tie Dylan to the crimes? But, really, this was Dylan. A jerk, yes. Arrogant, absolutely. She just had a hard time picturing him as a serial killer. Then again, she had a hard time picturing pretty much *anyone* as a serial killer.

She crept into Dylan's bedroom. He had a massive bed with—sure, why not?—black satin sheets that were turned down.

"What a tool," War muttered as he opened one of the nearby dresser drawers.

Her lips wanted to twitch as she glanced at him.

"*Rose.*" His voice was hard. Angry.

Her smile froze. "What is it?"

"Take a look."

She hurried to his side and peered into the drawer. The last thing she felt like spying was Dylan's underwear, but—she didn't see underwear in that drawer.

She saw a black morph mask. Just like the one the bastard who'd attacked her had worn. Her gaze locked on that mask, and she could not look away.

"Still think he couldn't be a killer?" War asked.

All of the blood seemed to be rushing away from her head. Rose sucked in desperate gulps of air. With a shaking hand, she reached for the mask. Her gloved fingers closed around it, and she lifted it up.

Pictures were tucked under the mask.

Pictures...of her. Of her running in the morning along the beach. Of her laughing as she had lunch along the pier. Of her kissing Dylan. *No, he kissed me. He set me up.*

He'd...tried to kill her?

But it wasn't just photos. There were three phones there, too. Burner phones. And the killer had been calling her. Taunting her.

"War." She looked up at him as her heart squeezed. What did they do now? How did they get the cops to see this evidence? The cops had to obtain it legally or it would be thrown out in a court case. If Dylan had killed those women, then she didn't want him walking. She wanted him rotting in a cell.

"Don't worry. I have a plan. Put it all back."

She slid the photos and the mask back into place. Started to push the drawer shut.

"Not all the way, baby." His fingers tangled with hers.

Her heart shoved hard in her chest.

"Leave it open. Just enough so that you can see that mask."

Her response was a jerky nod.

In moments, they were out of the house. He'd reset the alarm before they exited. They rushed to his car, and she flew into the front seat just before her jiggly knees would have given out on her.

*Dylan?* He'd done this? He'd killed those women and come after her? She couldn't quite wrap her mind around the horror that someone she knew, a man she'd worked with day in and day out, was a monster.

"Yeah. Yeah. You heard me right. Dylan Nelson's house. You need to do a search in there."

War's voice had her jerking back to the present. Her head swiveled toward him. He was talking to someone on his phone. She frowned at him.

His head turned. He met her stare. His eyes were cold. Hard. The darkness glinted. "You'll find evidence that will tie him to this mess." A pause. "What? Getting the search warrant is your department, not mine."

A search warrant? But...wait, was he talking to the cops? "War?"

"How the hell am I supposed to give you probable cause? Not like that was part of our deal."

Just who did he have a deal with? But the answer was there...because it was the only thing that made sense. *The cops.*

Yet...yet War had said he'd be working with *her*. That he'd give her forty-eight hours before he turned her over to the authorities.

Except now he was talking to someone— someone she thought must be a cop, and he was talking about their *deal*.

Betrayal burned through her.

"Don't look at me like that," War growled.

How was she looking at him? Like he'd lied to her? Set her up?

"No, no, dammit, I am not talking to you!" he fired to whoever was on the phone. "You have to get in that dick's house. What? Jesus, do I have to do everything? Fine. *Fine.* When security gets called, make sure you are on scene." He hung up the phone. Narrowed his eyes on Rose. "Do *not* look at me like that."

"How?"

"Like I freaking stole your favorite puppy, ate your last bit of cookie dough ice cream, and hid all the chocolate in the house from you."

Her lips wanted to tremble so she pressed them together. He knew cookie dough was her favorite, dammit.

"I did everything to protect you. Don't forget that." He curled his fingers under her chin. "I will continue to protect you. There is nothing I would not do for you. In order to keep you safe, I would lie, cheat, and kill. *Know it.*" Then he kissed her. A hard, angry brush of his mouth over hers.

Her hands lifted. To push him away—she was semi-sure that was her intention, but he backed away before she could. *Push him away...not pull him closer. Right?*

"Lock the car," he ordered flatly. "Do not leave until I get back."

"Where the hell are you going?"

His smile held a shark's edge. "The cops must have a reason to get inside. An alarm will send them rushing to the scene. And when they do go inside..." He tilted his head to the right. *Game on.* "They'll find that open bedroom drawer of his."

That was his plan? "War—"

"I'll be right back."

Then he was gone. Rushing for the house. Her fingers slid over the door handle. She thought about slipping out of the car. Running away.

*War lied. He was talking to the cops all along.*

She had to blink a few times. If she ran, where would she go? If Dylan was the one after her, if the cops could stop him and she could put this nightmare behind her...

*War lied.*

Why had she started to count on him? Why had she fallen back into her habit of trusting him so easily? Why? Why? *Why?*

But she knew the answer, even as pain pierced through her heart. She knew exactly why she'd been so willing to believe what War said to her.

Because, deep down, she still had a weakness for him. She still cared too much.

And because she cared, she hurt.

Her finger slid around the handle again and—

War ran toward her. He yanked open his door. "You didn't fucking lock it."

Rage poured through her. "*And you fucking lied to me.*"

He flinched. "Rose..."

"Are you working with the cops? Tell me the truth!"

He stared straight into her eyes—and nodded.

# CHAPTER NINE

"He says the mask isn't his. Says the phones aren't, either. According to Dylan Nelson, the guy has no idea how that stuff got into his drawer." The detective had taken off her coat and rolled up the sleeves of her white shirt. Detective Lynn Slater slanted a glance toward Rose. "Though he totally copped to the pics being his. Turns out, he is quite a fan of yours."

Rose's chin jerked up. "Not funny."

"No, I don't think anything about this situation is humorous. I tend to find dead women particularly unfunny." Lynn stared at her with hard, golden eyes. "You should have come to the police station sooner."

She knew Lynn. Their paths had crossed more than a few times as Rose covered the crime beat. But during most of those crossings, Lynn typically just said "No comment" and told Rose to get the hell out of her way.

Lynn's hair was cut short, sliding against her jaw. The cut made her golden eyes seem bigger. She was small, but Rose knew she could move fast when the situation called for it. Lynn hadn't been a detective very long, only two months since earning the promotion.

"I came to you before and told you about Barbara," Rose gritted out. "You didn't believe me, and she died."

Lynn tapped her pen against the side of the table. They were in an interrogation room. Lynn on one side of the table. Rose on the other. A silent War stood with his back pressed to the wall on the left. Rose didn't look at him. Not then. She was too busy trying to keep herself in control.

"You were tied to two murders, Rose. You knew the cops wanted to see you. You knew *I* wanted to see you."

Rose leaned forward. "I also knew that I had a killer on my trail. Someone who wanted me dead. I thought if I could find him first, then I could stop him from killing someone else."

"Hunting killers isn't your job," Lynn informed her crisply. "It's mine."

"Yes, well..." Rose offered her a brittle smile. "When I came to you before, you and your partner didn't seem so interested in *doing* your job. Where is Neal, by the way? Shouldn't he be skulking around and telling me that I'm in his way?"

"He took an early retirement. Now I'm in charge of the investigation, and I can assure you, things will be handled differently."

Rose straightened in her chair. Neal was gone? That was good news. He'd always given her a hard time.

"You're lucky that your boyfriend kept us in the loop." Lynn pointed toward a silent War.

Once more, Rose didn't look his way. "He's not my boyfriend. He's the PI who was hired to find me."

"Oh, is that what he is?" Lynn's eyebrows arched. "I see."

Why did this matter?

"Because of his intel, we were able to get to that motel off 61. I had a crew do a search there, but they didn't turn up much evidence we could use."

Back up. War had *sent* the cops to the motel? He'd been in contact with the cops even then?

"War assured me that you were being protected, and he told me he saw your attacker. He vouched for you being the victim, not the perp we were after. Though it would have been much more helpful to interview you at the time. Getting the facts about the attack directly from a vic is the way we normally operate. Instead, I had to get the details from War while you were, ah, resting, I believe you said it was?" Her stare cut to War.

He'd called the detective while Rose had passed out in his bed. Lovely to know.

Lynn's attention shifted back to Rose. "We were also able to catch your friend Billy before he ducked out of town. He told us about the visitor he had—the man who tried to kill him. Billy is talking plenty because he knows those warrants we have for him can make his stay with us very long."

Rose didn't let her expression alter. When she'd thought War had been talking to Odin, he'd been calling the cops. Talking to them right in front of her face. And she'd just blindly trusted him.

Her eyes closed. "How long are you going to hold Billy?"

"The DA is talking to him. Billy has quite a bit of information that will be useful to the PD. You know him, he always has stories to tell. I'm sure we will come to some sort of arrangement."

Yes, Billy did have plenty of stories. He knew where lots of bodies were buried.

Rose rubbed the nape of her neck. Knots twisted back there, and a dull ache pounded in her head.

"That's quite the bruise on your wrist," Lynn noted. "Want to tell me how you came to get it?"

She stared at her hand. She'd forgotten about it. "War cuffed me in the bathroom at the motel." Her words were hollow. "He didn't want me to run. He wanted to turn me over to the cops." *And he did.* Wasn't that why she was sitting at that table? So much for her forty-eight hours. "He left the motel room, and that's when the guy in the morph mask came in from the connecting room." She'd been in the station for *hours* answering questions, so she'd already told the cops this info. Woodenly, she went through the attack one more time. "I never saw his face because of the mask. He was tall, strong, about six foot—"

"Dylan's size."

"Yes." She exhaled. "He didn't say a word. I was too busy trying to stay alive to notice any other details about him. War came back inside, chased him off, and...then War took me home."

"Home?"

"His house. Where he called you and the two of you did whatever it is that you were doing." Her nostrils flared. "Are you going to be arresting Dylan?"

"We don't have enough evidence to do that."

She'd been afraid that would be Lynn's response.

"He *gave* us permission to search his house after the discovery of the mask, the phones, and the photos. We didn't find anything that would tie Dylan to the murders."

"You have the mask! It's the same mask—"

"That is sold in every novelty shop and costume shop in the world. My nephew has a mask just like it. Wore it last Halloween. Dylan having the mask doesn't prove anything."

Might not prove it, but it made him look guilty as hell in Rose's mind.

"What about the phones?" War asked.

The sound of his voice had Rose's shoulders stiffening.

Lynn's mouth tightened. "As far as we can tell, those phones have never been activated. We are looking at Rose's calls and seeing if we can track them, but it's not like we have any proof of what the perp said to her in those conversations."

Fury flashed in her. "I *told* you what he said. When I came to the station before Barbara died, I told you and your partner. I told you he was giving me clues, but you didn't believe me. You thought I was just some desperate reporter who was hungry for a story. You wouldn't listen to me." Her hands slapped on the table. "Barbara is dead. I wanted to help her. I wanted to save her. I couldn't. Then he turned his attention to me. I wasn't going to run to you and put someone else at risk. As long as I stayed out there, I knew he would search for me."

"And just how did you know that?" Lynn asked.

"Because that's what he told me." She wrapped her arms around her stomach. "I've been here forever." The day had been an endless blur of answering questions. "I want to go home."

"I told you, we can't arrest Dylan. I'm holding him as long as I can, but in a matter of hours, he'll be free, too. Going home won't be the smartest choice for you, not unless you have protection."

"She *has* protection," War said grimly.

Her head whipped toward him. As she'd feared, looking at him *hurt*. Her control splintered so hard she was sure that she heard the crack. Pain knifed through her heart. Why the hell had she trusted him?

"I will be with her." He stared straight into Rose's eyes. "She has me."

No, she didn't. She'd never had him.

"That will work," Lynn said, like everything had been all decided and tied up with a pretty, red bow. "You can keep reporting to me, and I'll—"

Rose shot to her feet. The legs of her chair scraped over the floor. "I'm going back to my job. To my life. If it's Dylan, then I'll do what I planned all along—*I'll* find enough proof to nail him to the wall." She stormed for the door.

Lynn stepped into her path. "I believed you," she said softly.

Rose stilled.

"My partner didn't. He's the one who was lead on the investigation. *Then*. Not now. I am not your enemy. I want to help you, and I want to find the man who is killing women in my state. We can work together on this. We can stop him."

She wanted him stopped.

"Do you believe Dylan Nelson is the perp?" Lynn pushed. "Do you think your producer is capable of killing?"

Until today, she would have said no. She *had* said no. Not Dylan. But... "Anyone is capable," Rose responded. "If pushed too far."

"Judging by the photos, he is quite hooked on you. In the pictures, you didn't look as if you knew that you were being photographed—"

"I *didn't* know."

"That worries me. Because if he's not our perp, he's still exhibiting stalking behavior that I find alarming."

Not like Rose found it all comforting and awesome. She was alarmed, too. She was also running way out of options.

But Lynn wasn't done being all grim and authoritative. "If you walk out of this station, you must have protection. Either police officers or your own personal guard." A wave of her hand back toward War before she told Rose, "I'm sorry, but I can't in good conscience let you just go out alone. If I must do it, I can have you taken to a safe house. I can have you put in protective custody—"

Basically held prisoner for who knew how long? No, not what she wanted. No, thanks. There was only one option from where Rose was standing. Even though that option pissed the hell out of her. "War," Rose bit off.

"Excuse me?" A furrow appeared between Lynn's brows.

"I'll go the personal guard route. I'll have War." She slowly turned to face him. He was still standing against the wall. His gaze immediately locked with hers. "I might not *like* you very much right now." Understatement. She wanted to scream at him because he'd hurt her, again. The bastard. "But I know you're more than capable of doing the job. You also hate Dylan, so there's that bonus."

"Fucking despise him," War confirmed.

"Yes, well, that means you should be able to protect me from him easily, doesn't it?"

He pushed away from the wall. "Damn straight I'll protect you."

"I'm sure we can work out an agreement about payment. You can bill me."

His gaze hardened. "I'll do it for free."

Oh, now he wanted to be generous? "Over my dead body."

He stalked toward her. "Never gonna happen."

As he got closer, her body tensed. Anger and fear and a dozen other emotions burned through her so that all she wanted to do was—

"Great. Wonderful. Glad this has been worked out." Lynn's voice was flat. "How about the two of you take yourselves and your weird tension out of my station? I need to go grill Dylan more before his lawyer shuts me down."

War didn't look away from Rose.

So she broke eye contact and spun for the door—and Lynn. "You'll keep us updated?"

"Of course. You do the same for me. If you see *anything* that sets off alarms for you, you contact me."

Rose nodded.

"We're going to be monitoring your phone."

*You should have done that before! When I came to you before Barbara died!* Her lips pressed together to hold back those words. Neal was gone. He'd been the one shutting things down. If Lynn wanted to work with her, if Lynn was going to be different, then Rose would cooperate.

"If this guy contacts you again, we want to know everything that he says. We will try to trace him and stop him." Lynn's gaze shifted to War. "I can count on you to continue keeping me in the loop? The same deal we've had before?"

Rose's hands fisted. How wonderful that they had a deal—wonderful for them. Painful for her.

Did War just make deals with everyone these days? Sure seemed like it.

"I won't let her out of my sight, and if someone comes for her, I will stop the SOB." A lethal promise.

Unease flashed on Lynn's face. "This isn't about you taking the law into your own hands. It's about guarding a victim."

"I will always protect Rose. Don't worry about that issue."

But he hadn't said a word about not taking the law into his own hands.

"And you..." Lynn pointed at Rose. "I'd prefer not to see you on the air talking about this case."

"I'm taking personal time. Not planning to jump in front of a camera any time soon."

Lynn didn't say anything else. She hurried out of the room and down the corridor—no doubt, going to grill Dylan. As Rose exited the room, her steps were just as fast as Lynn's. She wanted out of that place. Away from the ringing phones and voices and the sight of the desks covered with heavy case files that needed to be solved.

Before this nightmare, she'd loved working the crime beat. Since she'd become a target...

*Everything has changed.*

Rose hurried past the bullpen. Cut through the lobby. Shoved open the glass doors and burst outside. Night had fallen, and heavy darkness waited for her. The air felt thick and still, and she was far too conscious of War following right behind her.

His car was waiting on the other side of the street. Without a word, she headed for it. The traffic was light, so it was easy to dart across the road.

He reached the passenger side before she did. His hand slid out to curl around the handle. "You aren't looking at me."

No, she wasn't.

"You're barely talking to me."

It was good that he was being observant.

"Are you going to give me a chance to explain?"

"I don't want to do this on the street. I'm tired, and I want to get home."

He hauled open the door.

She sat down. Hooked her seatbelt. When Rose realized her fingers were shaking, she balled them into fists. Her control was definitely fracturing all over the place. She'd tried so hard to hold herself together. If she could just make it to her condo...if she could get inside, get to her bedroom. Lock the door...

Then she could fall apart.

He started the car. Pulled them away and drove slowly toward the intersection.

"*My* home," Rose emphasized. "I'm not going to your place. There is no way I'm sleeping in your bed tonight."

"If that's what you want..."

"It is. It is exactly what I want. That's why I said it." Her head turned so she was gazing out of the window. Her breath was coming too fast. Her chest ached.

"Rose, I did what I had to—"

"Could we just not talk for now? Let's drive in silence. Just...a little silence." A tear slid down her cheek. Angrily, she swiped it away. Breaking up with War the first time had hurt like hell. The same pain was hitting her again. The hollowness in her heart. The knots in her stomach. The pain that creeped and crawled through every part of her.

So much for being over him. If she'd been over War, then his lies wouldn't have hurt so much.

*He never had any intention of giving me forty-eight hours. He lied to me the entire time.*

# CHAPTER TEN

He had an emergency situation on his hands. As soon as they stepped into Rose's condo—and she immediately turned for the bedroom—War knew she was trying to shut him out. "I want to explain."

She took two steps forward. Stopped. With her back to him, she said, "I think I can sum up. You lied to me. You said you were going to give me forty-eight hours, but, instead, you were working with the cops all along. Talking on the phone to Lynn right in front of my face because I am such a trusting idiot where you are concerned."

"You are not an idiot."

Her shoulders squared. "You're right. I'm not an idiot. You're just an asshole." She strode for her room.

He surged toward her. He didn't spare a glance for their surroundings. He'd been in her home plenty of times before. Rose always had things perfectly in place. The condo was top of the line with an incredible panoramic view of the gulf. But he couldn't look anywhere but at her. His hand closed around her shoulder. "I didn't have a choice!"

"Sure, you did. You could have told me the truth at any point. Instead, you let me believe you had my back. You let me believe I could count on you." She huffed out a breath. "Would you stop touching me? I don't want you touching me right now."

All he wanted to do was touch her. Pull her into his arms. Make this shit right. But he instantly let her go. "Please, look at me."

She didn't.

"When you're really pissed with someone, you don't make eye contact." He'd noticed that about her. "It's like you can't stand to look at the person."

"You are not wrong."

His jaw locked. "I want you to look at me."

"I want to go to bed. Guess which one of us is about to get her wish?" Rose took four angry steps toward her bedroom door. Her hand pushed against the wood—

"Before I found you at Finch's, I had already contacted Lynn. Or rather, she had contacted me." He spoke quickly because he had to get this explanation out. He didn't want Rose mad at him. And he *hated* the pain he'd glimpsed in her eyes. "I've worked with her on a few other cases. She knows I can get the job done."

"How wonderful for her."

"I knew you weren't involved in the murders. You're not a killer."

"So...what?" Her hand still pressed to the door. "You took the case for shits and giggles? Because you just loved the idea of giving your ex a hard time as you shoved her at the cops?"

"I'm not going to pretend the initial image of you being at the police station didn't appeal to me." *Because I'm an asshole.* "I was mad. Hurt. But...shit changed fast. With you, it always does." His voice roughened. "Guess you never realized just how easily you wrap me around your little finger."

A bitter laugh slipped from her. "I don't think so."

"I do. I know so. When we were in that motel room, I knew right then that my plans were changing. *That* was why I walked out to my car and left you inside. I was trying to clear my head, but I was already a goner. You wanted my help? I was gonna give it to you. Then when I went back inside and saw that bastard attacking you..." A sight that would haunt him forever. "Nothing was going to stop me from protecting you."

Her head turned slightly in his direction, but she still wasn't looking *at* him. "How come you didn't come clean right then and there?"

"You didn't want to work with the cops. You still don't. I was afraid if I told you everything, you'd run." He swallowed. "Tell me I'm not wrong."

"You're not wrong."

War blinked.

"Doesn't mean I like it. In fact, I *hate* being lied to. I hate even more that I just fell for you so easily again that I let you do that to me and I—"

He lunged for her. Spun her around. "What did you say?" *She didn't want to be touched. Shit.* His hands fell once more.

Her gaze was on his throat. She wasn't meeting his gaze. Not even lifting her stare to his face.

"Rose. *Look* at me."

"You hurt me."

Her low voice was breaking his heart.

"I thought we were moving forward. That we could trust each other the way we hadn't done before, but you were lying to me every moment." She shook her head. "How is it so easy for you to lie?"

It hadn't been easy. Nothing about this damn case had been easy. Being so close to her, when he wanted her more than *anything* else in the world? Torture. "*Please.* Look at me."

Her long lashes slowly lifted.

"I am sorry." He could see pain in her eyes, and he *hated* it. "I didn't want you running, and I had to keep the cops involved because if I didn't, Lynn threatened to take you into custody." The same way she'd threatened earlier. "Keeping you safe is my number one priority. Hurting you wasn't part of my plan. It was never part of it."

"You didn't give me forty-eight hours. You said you would, but you didn't." Her lower lip trembled. "I thought we were a team."

"We are. I will keep working with you. We *are* going to stop him." There were tears gleaming in her eyes, and they made him want to promise her anything—everything—if he could just get those tears to vanish. "I will not let Dylan hurt you. I would kill anyone who threatened you."

"Don't say things like that."

Right. He was supposed to keep the darker part of himself separate from her. He'd done that before. Tried to push down who he really was because he'd wanted her so badly. In the end, he'd still lost her because others had known his weakness. "I'm a primitive kind of guy, Rose. A bastard. An asshole. I'm jealous and possessive—especially where you are concerned. When I got that pic of you and Dylan, it took all of my self-control not to immediately kick his ass." A long exhale. "And now, knowing that he might be behind all of this...knowing that he might try to hurt you..." She needed to understand this. "If he comes at you, I will stop him. No one hurts you on my watch. *No one.*"

"But *you* hurt me, War."

"God, baby..." Pain and guilt knifed through him. "I am so sorry." *Hurting you isn't what I want. What I want...it is you.* He wanted her back in his life. In his bed. He wanted her to look at him and smile. He didn't want to have her gaze cut away because she couldn't stand to see him. And when she did peer at him, War didn't want to find tears in her eyes. "I hate it when you cry."

"I'm not crying."

"No, of course not." He saw a tear leak down her cheek. "What can I do? How can I fix this?"

She took a step back. "Maybe we weren't meant to be fixed."

Bullshit. They were worth fighting for. *She* was. "I don't have other secrets. I'm not keeping anything else from you. You can ask me anything—from here on out—and I will tell you exactly what you want to know."

Shaking her head, she turned for the bedroom door once again. "I don't believe that."

"No?" He was desperate. "Try me. Fire any question at me. See what I say. Judge for yourself if I'm telling the truth or not."

Her gaze darted to him.

His head cocked to the right.

"Game on," she murmured.

War wasn't sure what she meant by that.

"Fine." Her hands went to her hips. "What did you think that first time when we met in your bar? You were all smooth and seductive. Was I another in a long line of pickups? Do you use the same routine on us all? Drop that oh-so-dramatic line of, 'I've been waiting for the night when you'd walk into my bar...' to all the ladies who catch your eye?"

He forced his jaw to unclench. She wanted honesty. He would give it to her. "I only used that with you, and it wasn't a line. I meant what I said."

"You'd been waiting for me?" Her tone mocked him. "You didn't even know me. How can you wait for someone you don't know?"

"Because, baby, I watched you every night on the news. I had the biggest crush of my life—on you. When you walked into my bar, there was no way I was going to let you leave without at least trying for a shot with you. My hands were sweaty. My heart was about to burst out of my chest. I felt like a freaking sixteen-year-old kid on his first date, but nothing was going to stop me from talking to you."

Surprise had her lips parting.

"Got more questions?" He motioned toward her. "Ask away."

"You wouldn't let me in."

His brow furrowed. "I let you in my home. My bar. Hell, I gave you *keys* to both places." Keys she still had.

"I mean—you wouldn't tell me about *you*. I did all the talking. Whenever I asked about you, you shut me down. Changed the subject. Got me naked. Whatever worked."

War took a moment to gather his thoughts on this one. "Just so you know, whenever I have the opportunity to get you naked, I'll be taking it. Having you naked with me is pretty much my favorite thing in the whole world."

Her eyes widened.

"But I changed the subject because talking about battles and death and people I couldn't save and lives that I had to take—I didn't want that to touch you. I don't like for anything bad to touch you. That's why I got so tense when you took the crime beat. I was worried about you. I didn't want you facing danger. I never want that. I guess that leads back to me being a bastard—where you are concerned, I am particularly greedy." Had been, always would be. "You see, I wanted you forever, Rose, and I didn't want anything to ever jeopardize you. I didn't want anything to scare you. Especially not my own past. I figured if you didn't know the things I'd done, then you couldn't be afraid. I thought I was finding a way to keep you close. Didn't realize until too late that it was just another thing pushing you away."

"How..." She stopped.

"Ask. Whatever it is, ask." He was desperate. Everything had changed when he saw her fighting for her life in that motel room—*everything*. When you realized how close you were to losing the person who mattered most, you fucking shifted priorities. He'd lied since finding her at Finch's, yes, but he had truly done it to protect her. For Rose, there was nothing he wouldn't do.

Her safety would always come first for him.

"How did you really feel about me when we were together?" Her voice was hesitant. Halting. "Was it just about sex?"

He closed remaining bit of distance between them. Her head tipped back as she stared up at him. "You have the most incredible eyes," he murmured. "I love the shade. I look into your eyes, and nothing else seems quite as important as you."

A furrow appeared between her eyebrows. "War?"

"The sex was amazing. No one else has ever come close to making me feel like you do. I lost control in bed with you. I didn't do that with anyone else. I could never get enough. I wanted you over and over again. If I had my way, I would have fucked you twelve times a day."

She licked her lower lip. "That's a lot of times."

His mouth curled. "Yes. And you had work, so I tried to be a gentleman." He lost his smile. "But I'm not very good at being a guy like that. I'm better at being the bastard who eliminates threats and kicks ass." He motioned to the perfect condo.

"That guy didn't fit so well in your world. He tried, but it wasn't his scene."

Her gaze darted around the condo. "I liked having you in my world."

*Baby, you are about to break me.* "I—"

"I should go to bed. My head is killing me, and I need some time to think."

He'd pushed enough. "I'll stay on the couch."

She turned away. "I have a guest room, if you remember."

He remembered everything about her.

"You can sleep in there. It's just a full bed, though, so it might not be long enough for you."

He'd take the couch. Not because the bed wouldn't be long enough. He didn't care about that. The couch's location put him closer to her.

She pushed open her bedroom door, but still didn't cross the threshold. She lingered, and War realized he was holding his breath as he waited for Rose to speak. But she didn't say anything. Just finally stepped inside, and War knew he was missing his chance.

*Fuck my pride.*

He bounded after her. Just as the door was swinging shut, his hand flew up to flatten against the wood. Surprised, she whirled toward him.

"I was falling in love with you," he told her flatly. "That's how I felt. That's why I lost my head when I got that photo of you and Dylan. I wanted you, only you, and I wanted you for keeps." His breath sawed in and out.

Her eyes were so wide.

God, he loved her beautiful gaze. "*Ask,*" he rasped because he could see the question on her face.

"What...what do you want right now?"

"I want the same thing I wanted before. You. Only you." He wanted her mouth. Wanted to kiss her and get lost in her and let the rest of the world fall away. He wanted to take and take and take, and he wanted Rose to do the same. He wanted the time that he'd lost with her—he wanted it back. "I want a second chance."

There. Done.

He shoved away from the door. "But for now, I'll be on the couch. You can sleep easy, sweet—Rose." Dammit, how many endearments had he been dropping? She didn't want him using those endearments. She'd told him that. "You're safe tonight."

She stared at him a moment longer. So many emotions were flying through her gaze. He held his breath.

She shut the door.

*Couch. Fucking couch. Get on it.*

\*\*\*

Rose stared at the door. *Second chance.* Her breath expelled slowly. He'd been all sexy and serious and downright lickable as he delivered his low, rumbling words to her. His dark eyes had burned with a sensual light as he'd said that what he wanted was—

*You. Only you.*

Her whole body was quivery. Her mind was in total chaos. She was furious with him. She *hurt*. And, dammit all to hell, she still wanted him, too. Nothing had changed that.

*I was falling in love with you.*

She wanted to believe those words. With all of her being, she wanted them to be true, but if he'd really loved her, would War have just let her go? Would he have lied to her this time about the forty-eight hours?

But as she considered the situation, Rose realized he hadn't said that he *loved* her. War had said—when they'd been together before—that he *was* falling in love with her. Falling was different. It wasn't the same thing as saying *I love you*. Was it?

She spun away from the door—the better to stop the temptation to yank it open and throw herself onto the couch and him. She stripped off her shirt. Kicked away her shoes. Shimmied out of the jeans and figured that even though she was bone tired, an icy shower just might do the trick—

A ringing stopped her. Froze her in place.

Her phone. It was in the heap of clothes she'd just carelessly tossed away. Her phone had been shoved in her back pocket. She bent, rummaged for it. As soon as she saw the screen— "*War!*"

The bedroom door flew back and slammed into the wall. He stood in the doorway, his broad shoulders nearly touching the frame, and his hands were fisted at his sides.

The phone rang again.

"I don't know the number," she said quickly. "This late—I think it's him!"

War rushed forward. "Put it on speaker. Answer him. Keep him talking as long as you can."

She knew she was supposed to keep the caller talking. The cops were monitoring her phone. War had pulled out his own phone and was firing off a text. Rose figured the text was either to Odin or Lynn or maybe to them both.

Her phone rang again.

He nodded.

Rose slid her finger over her phone's screen. Made sure to turn on the speaker option. "Hello?"

"He won't keep you from me." A low rasp.

Her spine straightened. "You're going to be locked away. You aren't going to hurt me or anyone else again."

"I enjoyed our time at the motel." Again, little more than a rasp. He was disguising his voice. Using one of those apps that anyone could download with the click of a button or just doing it old-school style.

"I can't say the same," Rose fired back. "My dream date doesn't involve some creep trying to strangle me with a bathroom towel. I'm more of a candlelight and champagne kind of woman."

"Is that what *he* gives you?"

Her gaze locked with War's. "He?" she repeated.

"I know he's there. So eager to run back to you. He thinks he can stop what's coming. He can't. I will have you."

"You aren't going to have anything but a life sentence behind bars. We *know* it's you, Dylan. You're making mistake after mistake after—"

He hung up.

She was almost crushing the phone. She immediately tried to call the number back. It just rang and rang. Exhaling slowly, she forced her fingers to ease their death grip on the phone. "Do you think they got him?"

War had his phone at his ear. His expression was so tense. So hard.

"Put it on speaker!" She wanted to hear everything that was said.

He jerked his head in a nod and lowered the phone. He hit the option for speaker and—

"You're sure that was him?" Lynn asked.

"Yes!" Rose said before War could reply. "He used the same rasping voice that he always uses. He said he had a great time with me at the motel— when he was trying to *kill* me. That was him! That was the killer!"

War's gaze shot to her. Dropped to her body. Whipped right back up.

*Oh, right. Standing here in my underwear.* She'd forgotten all about that. Other things had kinda taken precedence. *Like talking to a killer.*

"We got the call." Lynn's voice was stilted. "I have uniforms on the way now, and...you're not gonna like this."

What about this nightmare *did* she like?

"The call originated near your building."

Rose could feel the blood draining from her head.

"Stay inside," the detective ordered. "Lock the doors. Do not leave until you hear from me again."

A shiver slid over her.

"And—it's not Dylan."

What? Rose shook her head. "I didn't understand you." But she was afraid she had understood Lynn. *Repeat it, just in case.*

"I'm staring at Dylan Nelson."

Rose lunged for War's phone. "He just called me!"

"No, no, he did not. I still have him in an interrogation room. He is sitting at a table right now. I'm on the other side of the one-way mirror, and I can see him perfectly. Whoever called you— it was *not* Dylan Nelson."

A shudder worked over Rose's body. "That's not possible."

"I can assure you, it *is* possible. And holding him longer—not an option. His lawyer will use this development to get him out. He can't be in my interrogation room and be calling you at the same time. He's not the one we're after. He might be a sleaze, but it doesn't look like he's the killer." A rough exhale. "Uniforms are on the way, and I'm heading over, too. You stay where you are. Do not leave your condo. You got me?"

Yes, she got the detective. "I won't leave."

The detective hung up.

Another shiver slid over Rose's body. Maybe it wasn't just from fear. Maybe it was from the fact that she was standing there, only in her underwear, and she needed to get clothes on because War's hot stare was raking over her.

He tossed the phone onto the bed.

Rose tensed.

But he just strode for the bathroom. He came back out holding the pale blue, silk robe that she kept on the hook behind her bathroom door. "Here." He held it open for her.

She inched closer to him. Slipped it on. "Thank you."

He backed away. A big, giant step back. "He's not going to be there."

She turned to face him as she belted the robe.

"When they follow the signal, he'll be gone. Maybe he'll have left the phone somewhere close by. A little taunt for them and us. But no way the guy just sits like a good boy and waits for the cops to arrive." Utter certainty.

Unfortunately, she thought he was right. "How can it not be Dylan?"

A muscle flexed in his jaw.

"My stomach is in knots," Rose confessed. Her hand lifted to press to her throat. Oddly, she could have sworn the skin started to ache as she got the call. *It didn't, of course. I just remembered everything—*

His voice whispered through her mind. *I had a great time at the motel.*

War's gaze zeroed in on her neck. "It's bruised." He inched back toward her. Lifted his hand. His fingers skimmed lightly over her skin.

Another shiver shook her body. This one had nothing to do with the cold or with fear. As his fingers slipped over, Rose found her head tipping back. He leaned toward her. His mouth pressed to her throat. To the faint marks there. A tender, careful kiss. One. Then another. Another...

He pulled back. "Shouldn't have done that. Sorry." Curt. "I'll stay in the den. I want to do a perimeter check to make sure all of the doors are locked. You *are* safe, Rose. Know that." He spun and walked away.

She could still feel his mouth on her skin. Still feel him.

And she didn't want him walking away.

Rose wanted *him*.

\*\*\*

He wasn't interested in going up against the big, freaking bruiser she had playing guard dog for her. The bastard nicknamed War didn't interest him.

Rose was the one he wanted. The next victim. The woman who would not get away. Just as the others hadn't gotten away.

But the trick—it was to get *to* her. Rose was all locked away inside her condo. Like a princess in the tower of a castle. With a damn dragon guarding the door.

He had to get Rose away from the tower. Out into the real world. *Away* from the dragon.

He'd done that once before. He could do it again.

All he had to do was drive a wedge between them. Drive War away.

Then he could finish what he'd started with Rose.

# CHAPTER ELEVEN

"Figured that would be the case." Disgust roughened War's voice as he stared out into the night and took the call from Lynn. "I thought he'd ditch the phone and leave it as a present for us to find." He was on one of Rose's balconies, and the surf pounded below. The stars illuminated the beach—no one was out. Just an empty stretch of white sand.

"He's cocky," Lynn replied. "If he was right outside her place..."

"Then he saw me arrive with Rose. He knows I'm here with her. The last time he came for Rose, he waited for me to leave. The SOB likes to get his victims alone."

"And his victims are always women. He had the chance to kill Billy Angle, but he didn't. I'm thinking the perp did that because he doesn't get the same rush from killing men. Our perp has a type. He's locked and loaded on his next target."

"He won't get her." His gaze cut to the left. To Rose. She was on the balcony with him. Staring out as her robe blew gently in the breeze. The wind lifted her hair, too, tossing it back from her head.

"I have uniforms doing a sweep of the area. I'll be pulling any security footage that I can find. Maybe we'll get lucky and discover an image we can use."

Maybe. Maybe not. He didn't take his eyes off Rose. "You work your way. I'll work mine."

"War..." A warning edge had entered her voice. "I meant what I said before. This isn't about you killing the bastard. That had better not be the *way* you're talking about."

"Good night, detective. If you learn more, I'll expect to hear from you."

"I'll make sure a car is stationed outside. Don't do anything crazy, would you?"

He would make no promises because War felt absolutely *crazy* when it came to Rose. He hung up the phone. Shoved it into the back pocket of his jeans.

"Surprise, surprise." Rose wrapped her fingers around the top of the balcony's railing. "They didn't find him."

"Neither of us expected them to." He crept closer to her. He wanted to touch her. To skim his fingers down her arm. To pull her against him.

*I just want her.*

"Am I just supposed to go to sleep now?" Her head tilted as she stared into the distance. "Go to my bedroom? Act like everything is normal?"

"You need to rest."

"What I *need* is for that jerk to be caught. I was so sure it was Dylan. So sure." Her body was stiff. "Maybe it still is." She glanced toward him. "Maybe he got someone else to make the call so it would look as if he were innocent. That's a possibility. We have to consider it."

War already had. Still was. He nodded.

"My stomach is twisting. My heart won't stop racing. And I feel like I'm about to jump out of my skin."

He slid a little closer to her. "It's adrenaline."

"Before the call from him, I thought I could settle down. I was so tired but now, I'm wired." She turned to fully face him. "I'm scared."

He hated her fear. "I'm not leaving you."

"I haven't told my family. Not my parents or my sister. I don't want this touching them. Even if they found out, what would they do? They're down in Naples. They can't just rush up here and get in the middle of this mess. I have to protect them."

*And I will protect you.* He caught a lock of her blowing hair. Tucked it behind her ear.

She gave a little jerk.

"Sorry." His voice was rough. "Shouldn't be touching you." His hand started to lower.

Her hand flew up, and her fingers curled around his wrist. "I don't know what I'm supposed to do with you."

*Any fucking thing you want.*

"It's still there." Soft. He'd had to strain to catch her words.

"What is?" What was there?

"The need. The desire. You told me that you always wanted me. I feel the same way about you."

Okay, she could not say shit like that and expect him to keep acting like a gentleman. Just not gonna happen. She said stuff like that—and he wanted to fuck her on the balcony.

"I want you, War. Everything is crazy. *I* feel crazy. But the need is still there. I tried to make it go away when we broke up. I didn't want to think about you late at night. I didn't want to toss and turn and think about you. I wanted to make it all stop."

He'd never been able to stop thinking about her. "You starred in my dreams."

Her breath caught. "It's not normal to want someone this much."

"Says who?"

"I was hurt tonight. Furious with you. I shouldn't even be thinking about what I am..."

He leaned a little closer. "What is it that you're thinking about?" *Tell me, baby. Tell me everything.*

"Kissing you."

He thought about kissing her only every other moment.

"It's late. My emotions are a wreck. And I know a million reasons why we are a bad idea," Rose continued.

He didn't move. Neither did she. "You can go into the bedroom." His voice had roughened. "Shut the door. I'll take the couch."

"I could do that." A nod. Her fingers were still curled around his wrist. "Do you think it's possible to keep emotions separate from great sex?"

Maybe. But not for him. Not with her. If that was what she was asking for—a hard screw with insane pleasure so that she could take the edge off the adrenaline burn that was coursing through her—was that what he wanted?

Oh, who the hell was he kidding? Wouldn't he take her anyway he could get her? *In an instant.* "We can always try and see what happens."

Her hand slowly let his wrist go.

He dropped his arm. Brought his hands back to his sides. "Or you can go to bed," he said again. He was hard and hungry, and *trying* not to show how desperately he'd love to strip off her robe. Yank aside her panties. And take her against the wall as the surf pounded below them. "That's the...safer choice."

"Safe." A nod. "You're right. I'm sure that is the safer choice. Because in the morning, we don't want to wake up with regrets. An awkward morning-after situation and all that. There's enough going on without adding more drama to the mix."

He didn't speak.

She took a step back. Turned for the doors that would take her back inside. But she didn't actually advance toward those doors. "But the thing is..." Her husky voice was like a stroke over his body. Sensual. Seductive. "I want *you.*" Then she moved quickly. She came back to him. Shoved up onto her tiptoes, and her hands curled around his shoulders as Rose pulled him toward her. "And I don't want to think about how this is wrong."

Her mouth pressed to his.

*We're not wrong. Give me a chance. I'll show you how right we can be.* His fingers locked around her waist as his tongue met hers.

The kiss was hot. Hungry. Desperate.

Greedy.

Her taste was everything he wanted. Everything he could never forget. The wind blew against them. The waves thundered. Her nipples were tight and thrusting against his chest through the delicate silk of her robe. He wanted the robe gone. Wanted her bra gone.

Wanted her.

*Always.*

He lifted her into his arms. Held her easily as her legs wrapped around his hips. Her robe had ridden up, and only her panties were in his way. Her panties. His jeans. He didn't take his mouth from hers. War was enjoying the hell out of tasting her. He took a few steps toward the condo's doors, and he pressed her against the nearby wall.

It would be so easy to rip away her panties. To shove inside of her. To thrust deep and drive them both over the edge.

*In the morning, we don't want to wake up with regrets.*

Fuck.

Her body rubbed against his. Her nails bit into his shoulders.

*Here. Now.* He'd missed her. Missed the way she tasted. The way she smelled. The way she felt when her sex gripped him like the best paradise in the world.

But...

His mouth tore from hers. "We should...go inside."

She nipped his lower lip.

He jolted with hot lust. "Inside." He didn't let her go. He carried her back in. Paused only long enough to shut the door and flip the lock. Then he made his way to her bedroom.

His dick shoved against her with every step he took. She was sliding her core against the hard length. Driving his desire up to ever higher levels.

Making him want to take and take and never stop.

War lowered her onto the bed. He caught the belt of her robe and yanked it loose so he could see all of her.

Her panties and bra were so fucking sexy. But they were in the way. They needed to go.

He and Rose both pushed the robe aside. She fumbled with the back of her bra, and he tossed it to the floor as soon as the clasp was undone. He'd missed her breasts. Round and pert and with dusky nipples that he loved to lick.

He licked her nipple right then. Over and over. Licked and tasted and had her grabbing for the bed covers as she arched up against him.

His legs were between hers. He spread her thighs wide as his fingers trailed down her body. He pushed his hand against the crotch of her panties as he kept up his sensual play with her nipple. Her panties were wet. She was arching into his touch. Moaning his name. Giving him everything he'd wanted—

*No regrets.*

He stroked her through the panties. She squirmed against him. Her breath panted out.

He began to kiss his way down her body. He wanted to kiss every single inch of her. Her body had always driven him crazy. So he just had to taste all of her.

Her thighs opened more for him. He used his index finger to trace lightly over her sex, through the panties.

"You are teasing!" Rose cried out.

No, he wasn't. When it came to her, he didn't tease. He was dead serious. His hands moved to either side of her hips.

"War?"

He curled his fingers around the lace along her hips and just ripped the panties and tossed them out of his way.

Better. Much better.

He put his mouth on her. Her hips surged up against him. He licked her. Sucked. Kissed. Thrust his tongue over her clit and then into her core. She was arching and grabbing for his shoulders, and her taste was just driving him on. Making him hungrier. Wilder. Rougher.

*"War!"* Her whole body tightened. He could hear the pleasure in her voice as she called out his name.

The first orgasm. He greedily tasted that release. And worked her with his fingers and mouth until he could send her crashing into a second.

When that second wave hit, a tremble rocked her. Her nails and fingers pressed harder against him, and she whispered his name.

He licked her again. Tenderly. He *loved* the way she tasted.

His head lifted. He stared up at her and knew he'd never wanted anyone more.

Her eyes met his. Slowly, he slid back. Moved to the side of the bed. He stood, and his hands went to the snap of his jeans.

*I want to drive into her. Sink as far as I can go. Find oblivion and pleasure and mark her in a way that proves we are far from fucking over.*

Her breath came quickly. His gaze drifted to her breasts. Those perfect breasts.

Then down, down to the sex he'd just licked.

He reached forward—

And pulled the covers they'd somehow kicked aside up *over* her body.

"War?" Confusion trembled in her voice.

"Can't have you waking up with regrets tomorrow." He'd be the one doing that. Kicking himself. Calling himself a dumbass for the move he was making. And it hurt. Like, freaking hurt because he was so turned on and all he wanted to do was plunge inside of her.

One of her hands grabbed the cover as she shot into a sitting position. "You're walking away from me?"

He was heading for an ice-cold shower. Then the couch. "I don't want just tonight."

She shoved back her hair. "What is happening right now?"

*I'm trying to be a good and not jump you like I'm starving.* "You're coming off an adrenaline rush. Your emotions are all over the place. In the morning, you might be back to hating me. I...don't want that." Her hate was the last thing he wanted. "So maybe...when you wake up, you'll realize that I'm not always a total ass. At least not with you. Other people can go fuck themselves, but with you...*I'm different.*" Did she get that? Did she understand what he was trying to do even as every single part of his body protested?

He was putting her first. For him, she had to come first. Hell, literally. He'd made sure she came—twice—but he wasn't going to find his own release. He was doing something for her. Proving that he was more than an arrogant, jealous ass and a liar and—

"Shower," War rasped. A nipple had just peaked out at him. He was at the end of his rope. If he didn't get away from her, now, his good intentions would go straight to hell. "Good night, Rose."

He whirled and marched for the bathroom. He shut the door behind him and immediately began to strip. His dick bobbed up in the air, obviously not fucking pleased with his life choices.

War wrenched on the shower water and stepped under the icy spray.

\*\*\*

"No." Rose stared at the closed door. He wasn't doing this. Wasn't going to give her so much pleasure that she had splintered apart and then walk away. She'd seen the need on his face. The savage lines of hunger.

He'd wanted her.

She still wanted him.

And it darn well wasn't about some adrenaline rush and crazy emotions. When it came to War, she'd always wanted him.

Rose slung aside the covers and rushed for the bathroom door. She twisted the knob—he hadn't locked the door—and threw it open. As she stormed inside, she kicked past his discarded clothes. "*War*." Angry. Determined.

He was in her shower. The water thundered down on him. His back was toward her, but she could see him clearly through the glass shower door. No steam drifted from the water—she knew it was probably ice cold, just as he'd said.

"You don't want to do this," he warned. His hands pressed to the tiled wall in front of him. "Walk away, Rose."

She walked closer. "I want you."

The water trailed down his body. Slid over his strong, muscular back. Down that awesome ass of his. Truly, the man's ass was great. And those powerful legs and those—

He swung around toward her.

*Huge*. Massive. His cock bobbed toward her. "The cold water isn't helping," he growled. "And you standing there naked...*I'm trying to be good*."

"Oh, War..." She opened the door. "You're way better than good in bed, and we both know it." She stepped beneath the spray. Gasped because it was *freezing*. Her nipples pebbled hard and her stomach sucked in. But she didn't retreat. Her hand rose to press to his chest—his cold, hard chest. "Turn the water off," she breathed as she stood onto her tiptoes and pressed a quick, hungry kiss to his lips. "And fuck me."

He wrenched the water off. Yanked her up into his arms and pushed her against the wall. He caged her there even as this cock shoved toward her—

He stilled with the head of his cock lodged at the entrance to her body. "Condom." Another growl.

"I'm still on birth control. There hasn't been anyone since you. I'm clear. I'm—"

*"There hasn't been anyone for me since you."* His eyes blazed with dark fire. "There never will be." He sank deep.

That was it. She was lost. All control stripped away. His cock stretched her and had her moaning and they were *wild*. He pounded into her. Her hands held onto his shoulders for dear life. She didn't feel the cold any longer. How could she? Her heart was nearly bursting from her chest. Her breath heaved in and out. Her legs had locked tightly around his hips. Each deep thrust had her arching into him.

His cock filled her. Over and over. Slid in and out. She pushed up so she could look down at them—

*Oh, God.*

He held her with his right hand. Such easy strength. His left slid between their bodies. Stroked her. She watched. She—

Came so hard that she thought she just might pass out. The pleasure slammed through every cell in her body. Rose couldn't cry out at all. She was too busy soaking in the release and letting it fill every hollow, dark spot inside of her. The climax kept pouring through her. Not some little peak—there were no little peaks of pleasure with War. More like a non-stop onslaught that was wrecking her world and leaving her shaking and satisfied and...

He drove deep once more. Erupted inside of her. Her hold on him tightened even more. She forced her eyelids to lift—they'd closed when her release first hit. She stared at him. Saw the savage beauty of his face as pleasure washed over his features.

He looked back at her. His eyes stared straight into her soul. And he just said... "Mine."

***

Dylan Nelson shoved open his front door. He'd been at the station for too damn long answering all of those ridiculous questions from the cops. His lawyer had told him that cooperating was in his best interest.

He probably should hire a new lawyer. That prick had been getting on his last nerve.

He glared around the house. He'd told the cops they could search his home. He didn't have anything to hide in his place. Not like he was keeping freaking kill trophies under the bed or something.

He needed a drink. Maybe two. He'd been grilled like some kind of criminal. He was a respected producer. He had a wall full of awards. Hell, he'd been recognized by the mayor last year because of the charitable shit he'd done.

Yanking at his tie, Dylan headed for the kitchen. He was almost there when his phone vibrated in his pocket. He hauled it out and peered down at the screen.

When he saw the text sender's name, his jaw clenched. His finger slid across the surface of the phone. Gary had still been tailing War. But now that Rose wasn't hiding any longer, that job would end. It would—

Dylan frowned.

Gary had sent him new photos. He clicked on them. Made them bigger. Dylan swallowed and glared as the shots appeared.

*War.* Kissing Rose. Pressing her up against that stupid old car of his.

*War.* Putting his hands all over Rose. Acting like he fucking owned her or something.

Why the hell had she fallen for that asshole? Why was she letting him touch her again?

Why couldn't she learn from her mistakes?

The phone vibrated again as a text appeared. *Do you want me to continue surveillance?*

He fired off a quick response. "*Send me a bill. Your job is done.*" Gary had handled several jobs for him in the past. The PI had always been discreet, and he delivered exactly as promised. He could get dirt on anyone. A useful trait in the media world.

Dylan hesitated. Actually...maybe Gary *could* still be useful. Before, Dylan's goal had been to get War angry enough to turn from Rose. But maybe Rose should be the one turning away. Maybe she didn't know her boyfriend as well as she thought. Perhaps no one did. "*Change of focus,*" he texted. "*Dig up everything you can on Warren Channing. I want every single skeleton he has.*"

Three little dots appeared on his screen. Dylan waited...

The response: *Done.*

# CHAPTER TWELVE

Her phone was ringing. Rose cracked open one eye as the peal of sound penetrated the deep layers of sleep. She threw out her hand—aiming generally for the direction of the noise—but instead of hitting her nightstand, she hit a warm, hard body.

*War.*

Her second eye opened. She found him staring back at her.

"Morning," he told her in his deep, growly, I-just-woke-up voice. A voice that had her wanting to squirm because it was pure sex appeal.

The phone rang again.

"I need to get that." She leaned over him, kind of *crawled* on top of him, and scooped up the phone. It had been the standard ringtone, so she didn't realize who the caller was until she glanced down and—"Dylan."

Beneath her—because she was almost straddling him at this point—War stiffened. "What the hell does he want?"

Since she hadn't taken the call yet, Rose had no clue. Her breath huffed out and her finger tapped the screen. "Dylan?" She made sure to put the call on speaker so War could hear, too.

"We need you. Get to the station, *now*."

What? That was the way he greeted her after everything that had happened? "I'm on leave. Find someone else."

"Your leave is up. Jeremy just broke his leg water skiing, so he can't go on air. The cops found a female homicide victim on the beach this morning, and we need a reporter on site. *You* are in charge of the crime beat."

A female victim? "What happened to her?"

"I don't know. How about you do your job and find out? Get to the station. I'll have a crew waiting for you—"

"No."

"Excuse me?" His voice rose. "Is your job not worth—"

"I'm at my condo. It makes no sense for me to drive to the station, then come back to the beach. Give me the location. I'll go straight to the beach and meet the crew there."

She heard him swiftly inhale. He didn't like her plan. Too bad.

"Fine," he snapped. "But when you get the segment filmed, you come back here. We need you to stand in for the anchor tonight."

Seriously? "Am I standing in for everyone?"

"Thought you wanted a shot like this. Thought you'd be *happy*."

War stared up at her.

Her heart drummed and echoed in her ears. "Finding out that you've been keeping creepy pictures of me hardly makes me happy. If this anchor slot is just some bribe you're doing so I won't report you to the station manager, you need to think again."

"Rose—"

"I'll come to the station, I'll do my job, but you're going to be answering plenty of questions for me. *And* for the station manager."

"You were wanted in connection with a murder investigation. You dropped off the radar! Do you really think the manager is going to take your side on anything—"

"I guess we'll find out." Her voice was way calmer than she felt. "Text me the exact location for the body." There were miles of beaches around her. "Good-bye, Dylan." Once more, her finger tapped on the screen.

She put the phone back on the nightstand. Realized her legs were on either side of War's body. He hadn't said anything during her conversation with Dylan, but he'd heard every word.

As she sat perched on him, Rose became aware of—

*Oh, hello. Good morning.* "I should move."

His hands came up and closed around her thighs. "You should stay exactly where you are."

Ever so tempting. But she'd just realized she was stark naked. A thin sheet was the only thing stopping that heavy morning erection of his from thrusting right inside of her. And *why* did she just wiggle against him?

"You were cool to that bastard."

And War sounded cool as he was talking to her. Like they were just having an easy morning talk. Not like he was sporting a massive hard-on and she was naked on top of him. Was this how things were supposed to be? Was she supposed to pull off some casual, oh-sex-is-nothing bit? Because that wasn't her. She didn't sleep around. When she slept with someone, she did it because that person mattered.

The fact that she'd jumped into bed with War so soon after they'd met—maybe he'd gotten the way wrong idea. For her, it hadn't been casual.

*I was in over my head. I knew he could be the one. I knew I'd never felt that way before.*

"Surprised you didn't tell him to go to hell." That deep rumble probably wasn't supposed to be sexy—but it was.

"I intend to do that, but I want to question him first." She started to ease to the side. His hold tightened on her. "War?"

"Thought you told Lynn you weren't going on the news."

"I'm not going to talk about the man after me." That was what she'd agreed to do. Not talk about the case that involved her.

"No?" His fingers pressed into her skin. Was he arching? Was his cock pushing against her? Or...was she pushing against him? "Don't you think viewers will wonder what's up? You've been named a person of interest in a murder and bam, now you're all of a sudden back on TV."

"I'll think of something to explain my absence." When she could think. Something difficult to do in her current position so—

She pulled away. Climbed from the bed. Ignored her shaking knees. "A victim has been found. I need to make sure the perp after me—

that he didn't take another woman in my place."
She needed more details about the death. Her
phone vibrated on the nightstand. She glanced at
the address. "That's about three miles away." *So
close.*

"You know I'm coming with you."

"I expected nothing less." Having a
bodyguard watching her ass? Yes, please.

He sat up. Slowly. She tried not to let her gaze
dart to his chest. She failed. Rose shoved back her
hair. "I have to get dressed. The crew will meet us
there."

He caught her wrist before she could turn
away. "Is this the awkward morning-after
situation?"

Her brow furrowed.

"The one you feared would happen if we gave
into the overwhelming urge to fuck each other."

My, my. War was blunt in the morning.

"Is that why you aren't talking about what
happened?" His fingers were lightly caressing the
inside of her wrist, moving tenderly along the
faint bruise that still marked her skin from the
cuffs. "You regret it?"

Rose shook her head. "Not for a second."

His nostrils flared. "Good." A pause. "You're
giving us a second chance?"

Is that what she was doing? "I don't know."
Honest. "I just know that I've never reacted
normally to you. The way you can make me feel—
it's more intense than anything I've ever
experienced. My control is never what it should be
with you." But he didn't seem to have that
problem. After all, he'd been the one to put his

mouth all over her and then walk away as he headed for the bathroom and shut the door ever so softly behind him. Meanwhile, her whole body had still been quaking. "I have to get dressed," Rose repeated. She tugged her hand free. Hurried into the bathroom. This time, she was the one to shut the door. Ever so softly. But then she glanced toward the mirror. Saw her wide eyes. Her flushed cheeks.

*What have I done?*

But deep down, she knew. Rose was...She was...

Hell, she was in trouble.

***

War watched as Rose talked to her crew. By the time they'd arrived, the body had already been transported. But it hadn't taken Rose long to get the scoop on what had gone down. It appeared that the woman was a drowning victim. *Not* a homicide victim. She'd been found in her bathing suit, washed ashore, with no signs of trauma on her body.

The rip currents in the area were dangerous bastards. War knew they had taken more than their share of victims, and if the woman had gone out for a swim under the moonlit sky...she might not have been prepared for what waited on her.

But it wasn't time to make that judgment yet. The ME would do an exam. The cops would conclude their investigation.

War heard someone say, "Going live." He backed up and watched Rose. She squared her shoulders and looked straight into the camera.

*"I'm on the scene at a local beach where a body was discovered by a jogger shortly before—"*

"Thought she wasn't getting back in front of the camera."

War didn't look away from Rose. He'd been aware of Odin's slow approach. He'd caught sight of his friend from the corner of his eye.

"At least, that was the message you texted me last night."

"Dylan called her this morning. The ass seems to be threatening her job. Told her she had to show up. The guy who *should* have been filming broke his leg." He kept his voice low. "Our next stop is the news station, and I can guarantee you, I will be having a nice, long talk with the jerk."

"The vic on the beach wasn't strangled."

Now War did glance Odin's way.

The blond shrugged. "I did some digging. Actually arrived at the scene before you did. When I heard on the scanner about the body being discovered—a female victim, so close to Rose's place—I wanted to make sure the guy we're after didn't strike out at someone else."

Wasn't that what they'd all feared?

"No wounds were on her neck. At least, not that I saw. I got a few more details from the cops before they me shut down, but this death seems unrelated. A fucking tragedy..." His gaze swept toward the waves. "But not a murder by our guy."

Rose was still speaking as she motioned toward the waves.

"Got my tech friend to try and learn more about the photo sent to you. He's working on it but—"

"I figured out who sent it." War had just forgotten to tell Odin. "A PI named Gary Strom. Real piece of work. He likes to peer in windows and take pictures of people."

Odin rocked back on his heels. "Want me keeping an eye on him?"

He measured his buddy. "I'd appreciate it." He wanted to say more. To ask how Odin was doing. This was the first time that Odin had actually appeared *interested* in working on anything lately. He'd been drifting too much. Living in the past and the pain there. "I could use a partner on this case."

Odin's blond brows rose. "Partner?"

"If you're going to be sticking around town, maybe you should consider joining the PI business with me. Clients have been increasing, and I need the help." The PI side business had started as a hobby. War had been used to spending his days and nights in battles. Giving up the adrenaline, suddenly being a civilian who didn't live on the edge—it had been one hell of an adjustment.

So he'd looked for something to capture his attention.

Decided to try a few side gigs. Discovered he had a knack for the job.

Odin didn't reply. War figured that meant his friend was thinking things over. He wouldn't push. Odin wasn't the type of man you could push.

War's attention shifted back to Rose and her crew.

"Got it!" The cameraman backed up after making his announcement. "I'll take a few scene shots, but we should be good here."

Rose blew out a breath and nodded.

"She ok?" Odin asked.

"Rose is a lot stronger than she looks."

"Good to know." Then, "*You* ok?"

*No, man, I'm falling in deep again, and I don't know what the hell I'll do if she walks on me.* "Great. Couldn't be better. Fantastic."

"Shit. You had sex with her."

Those words—accurate words—had his stare whipping back to Odin. "Don't push on this. Don't say anything that makes her feel uncomfortable."

Odin rubbed his chin. "I was doing a little spring cleaning at your place."

Talk about a conversational change, but... "Since when?"

"Found something interesting in your kitchen drawer. Seemed weird, you know, having an engagement ring shoved in with your spoons."

*Fuck.* His buddy had found that? A swift glance to the right showed Rose closing in. "*Not a word.*"

"Left it there. But you might want to move it, you know, if you're planning on having company—other than me—over soon."

Yes, he made a mental note to do just that. *Move the ring.*

"Drowning victim." Rose exhaled on a long sigh. "I learned that she'd checked in to a hotel on the beach just two days ago. She's here with her sister." Rose looked toward the water.

He could see the sadness on her face. The stories got to her. The people did. He knew it. He'd witnessed it plenty of times before when he watched her reports on the news. Emotion would quaver in her voice. Pain would flash on her face. That was the thing about Rose—she actually cared. No *if it bleeds, it leads* bullshit with her. The people mattered.

That was why he knew the murder of Barbara Briggs must have ripped her apart.

But as he watched, Rose straightened her shoulders. Her gaze darted to Odin. Her left brow quirked. Her lips parted—

"Odin has a new job," War told her quickly. *Do not mention the ring.* He would cross that bridge soon enough. "He's gonna be keeping an eye on our buddy Gary."

"The PI?" She blinked.

"Um. I don't like the guy. Like it even less that he's so tight with Dylan. I think we need to examine his life a little bit more." A hell of a lot more.

Odin gave a quick salute. "On it." He turned and walked across the sand.

Rose pulled out a pair of oversized sunglasses and perched them on her nose. "Does he talk more when it's just you and him?"

Ah...about that. "Odin is shy."

"Right."

"No, seriously, he is. Growing up, Odin was always bigger than everyone else. Stronger. He was always worried about hurting people who were weaker than he was, and when it came to girls..." He shook his head at the memory. "The man still can't talk well with them. He says awkward shit when he tries. Does awkward shit. So he now has a method where he says as little as possible." A wince. "By the way, that's why he screwed up with you that first night. I know he sounded like a dick, but he was trying to look out for me, in his way."

He couldn't see her gaze, but her head had angled toward Odin's departing form. "But he said he was the charming one."

Another wince. "I told him he was charming. That he *could* be charming. Trying to build up the guy's self-esteem, you know? He had a tough time of it on the last mission." Memories Odin didn't want to face. "And now he's here and alone—"

"He's not alone." Considering. Quiet. "He has you."

*Damn right, he does.* "I don't care about blood, that man is my brother. I'd do anything for him, just like he'd do the same for me." No hesitation.

"Then I will very much try to see his charming side."

He squinted at her, but her voice wasn't mocking.

"If he inspires so much devotion, then I am sure the man has many good points."

"When the other kids picked on me..." *Why was he telling her this?* He'd kept so much from her because War didn't usually see the point in revisiting the past. But maybe...keeping all that from her had been the reason they didn't make it the first time. "Other kids gave me a rough time. Called my dad a loser. Said no one wanted me. But Odin was there. When they came at me, he stood between me and them until I was strong enough to fight my own battles."

Once more, her head turned as she seemed to look after Odin. But he was gone.

"We should go, too," War murmured. "There are some things at your station that I need to take care of."

"Things *you* have to take care of? Are you going to share with the group?"

The group?

"Me," Rose clarified.

War winked. "Figured that." He stepped closer to her. His knuckles slid over the edge of her cheek, just beneath the sunglasses. "You are so beautiful."

Her breath caught.

"It's payback time." She should be aware of this. "I've been good as long as I could be, but those photos—the dick's obsession with you..." His teeth ground together. "Knowing that Dylan hired the PI to break us up...yeah, that shit can't go unpunished."

Her body had tensed. The wind picked up a lock of her hair and tossed it across her forehead. "What are you going to do?"

"I think Odin's mom would say I'm gonna have a come-to-Jesus meeting with him."

"What?"

He smiled. "He crossed the line. He doesn't get to do that." *He doesn't get to stalk you. Doesn't get to make you feel uncomfortable or scared or any damn thing.*

"War—this isn't the time to go all alpha, jealous angry on me!"

He thought it was precisely the time to do that. But... "I'm not jealous. I trust you. Completely." She should understand that. "This is about making sure he gets a message."

"What message would that be?"

"That he doesn't fuck with you and he doesn't fuck with me." Simple enough. "And there's a price to pay." His hand fell away from her cheek.

*Her* hands immediately flew up to press against his chest. "Don't do something crazy. If you wind up in jail, what will I do?"

"Aw, Rose...sounds like you're getting sweet on me again."

"Sweet?" The one word was sharp. "Did you just say that to me?"

He had. "I won't go to jail. Don't worry." Not his first rodeo. "But I do think it might make things infinitely easier for us if Dylan was cooling his heels in a cell for a while."

"War..."

"Have I mentioned how insanely beautiful you are?"

"You...you are trying to distract me."

Maybe. He was also telling her the truth. "I don't know if I tell you enough, but I think you're the most beautiful woman I've ever seen in my life."

"Oh, God." She gulped. "You're going to do something incredibly dumb or dangerous, aren't you? You're trying to butter me up so I won't completely lose my mind when you do said dumb or dangerous deed." Once more, the wind blew her hair. "Not going to happen. I will lose my mind if you get in trouble. I don't want you getting locked up for me. Dylan isn't worth it, understand? Keep that iron-clad control of yours around him."

Dylan wasn't worth jack. But *she* was worth everything. "I will keep my control." He would be perfectly in control. It was Dylan who wouldn't be. "Don't worry."

Rose winced. "I am worried. Very worried."

He leaned down and brushed his lips over hers. "Being worried...does that mean you forgive me for working with the cops?"

Her body leaned into his. "Did you ask for my forgiveness?"

Another kiss. She tasted delicious. But he forced his head to lift. "Will you forgive me?"

Her hands still pressed to his chest. Her mouth was so close. He should kiss her again. He should—

"No. I will absolutely not forgive you, but if you don't do something dangerous and crazy with Dylan, we'll talk. Revisit that whole forgiveness idea." A firm nod. "Time to go."

Cute. But no deal. He was going to absolutely do something dangerous and crazy to Dylan. The bastard deserved it.

*I should have kicked his ass when I first got the picture of him putting his mouth on her.*

The way War saw it, he was just taking care of unfinished business.

# CHAPTER THIRTEEN

As always, the news station was a buzz of activity. War had been to the station before when he'd come by to pick up Rose, so several of the people there—including a security guard munching on a donut—gave him a friendly wave.

Rose had vanished into a closed-door meeting with the station manager. War was using the time he had to do a little recon work. And the best way to do recon work?

With delicious donuts.

"Cordell, nice to see you," he greeted the guard near the front desk. "Tell me those don't have lemon inside. I'm not a filling guy."

"Only pure glazed deliciousness." Cordell lifted the box toward War.

"Don't mind if I do." He helped himself. While he was munching, he casually swept his gaze over the sign-in log. "Gary Strom..." He drew out the name. "Isn't that the creepy PI who takes pics of cheating spouses? What's he doing coming here?"

"Dude *is* creepy." Cordell nodded. "But he's tight with Dylan. Got to always let him in when he comes. Standing orders."

Interested now, War swallowed down the last of his donut. "Just how far back do those two go?"

Because he'd thought Dylan had just hired Gary for recent work.

"Since before I started here. That was about a year and a half ago. Dylan gave me those orders on day one."

Good to know. "Any problems at the station lately? Anyone causing trouble? Trying to get inside when he or she shouldn't?"

Cordell's face scrunched as he seemed to think about it. "Not really. It's been pretty quiet. Our biggest drama was Rose being suspected of murder."

"She didn't kill anyone." A too-fast retort.

"Of course, she didn't. It's *Rose*. Everyone loves her. She's not like those other arrogant pricks who snap orders all the time. Rose is the real deal. What you see is what you get with her."

He leaned closer to Cordell. "Do me a favor?" He slid cash across the counter. "Make sure you keep an extra watch on Rose."

"Don't need money to do that." Cordell slid the money right back toward him. "And just what should I be watching for?"

"Some bastard paying too much attention to her."

The nearby doors swung open. Dylan strode across the lobby.

"There's the bastard who does that," Cordell told him softly.

And Dylan was just the bastard War had been waiting to see. Before Dylan could rush by and escape into the production area, War stepped into his path.

Dylan pulled up short, then immediately moved to the right.

So did War.

Dylan took a step to the left—

As did War. He smiled. *I can do this all day. Let's dance, motherfucker.*

"You're in my damn way!"

"Am I?" War feigned shock. "Maybe then...if you want me *out* of your way, you should do something like...I don't know...kiss my girlfriend—when she has *zero* interest in you—and get your sleazy friend to photograph you. Then you can send the photo to me because—"

"Not my fault you're a jealous prick!" Dylan fired back. "Controlling and dangerous. And a *killer!*"

War let his eyebrows rise.

"How many lives did you take while you were a SEAL? How many times did you get sent out because you were the one who seemed to thrive on death?" Dylan's eyes were practically shining as he loudly threw out the charges.

War heard a door open behind him. The door that led back to production. But he didn't take his gaze off Dylan to see who'd just entered the lobby.

"You came back home and tried to run your shithole bar." Dylan sneered at him.

A shithole, huh? "Seems like a popular enough shithole to me. Don't hear lots of complaints. Just see a long line of folks eager to get in."

"You tried to stop fighting, but you were addicted to the bloodlust. Messed up on the inside. So you started working cases even the cops didn't want to touch. Slumming it with criminals."

"I don't slum it with anyone. Thanks for asking."

"Breaking laws to get what you wanted! You were already over the line, sinking in deep. Deemed too dangerous to be in the field any longer, you came back *here*. And then you just turned all of those pent-up emotions loose. You were a ticking bomb waiting to explode. Not my fault if you saw a picture of Rose enjoying time with me and you lost it—"

A sharp gasp from behind War.

Dylan's attempt to provoke him was cute. In a sad, annoying-as-fuck way. Dylan thought he could push War's buttons. *Not this time.* "Been doing some digging, have you?"

The SOB looked so pleased with himself. "Gary told me a thing or two about you."

Just how had Gary come up with that intel so quickly? A point to analyze later. For now... "I did some digging of my own."

He'd been busy during the night. Too wired to sleep, he'd turned up a surprising amount of information once he started digging—and calling in favors from sources. "Does your boss know about that arrest you got when you were in Atlanta last year?"

Dylan's lips parted. He blinked. "That was a mistake."

"That was solicitation of a prostitute." He made sure his voice was nice and loud. Just like Dylan's had been. *Yeah, I get we have an audience. I can work a crowd, too.* "And it wasn't the first time you tried to pay for services. Same thing happened to you the year before. You just can't distinguish between undercover cops and the real deal, can you? Busted *twice*."

"Lower your voice!"

He raised it. "Two solicitation charges. I would think stuff like that would be big news. Breaking news, if you will. I am sure the station manager would love to know all about—"

"Shut your fucking face!"

Oh, Dylan was getting angry. Not angry enough. Not yet.

"Is that why you were trying to force your attention on Rose?" War asked as he tilted his head to the right. *I am taking your ass down.* "Because you usually have to pay for a woman to spend time with you? Rose wasn't interested. She told you to back the hell up, but you wanted—"

Dylan swung at him. War took the blow. A necessary act. And, hell, it was one bullshit blow. Barely even clipped him on the chin.

"*War!*" Rose's worried voice. Her heels tapped across the floor.

He'd figured she was the one who'd left production.

She curled her fingers around his shoulder. "War, are you okay?"

"Fucking fantastic." He wanted to smile at her, but he wasn't done.

"He's *fine*." Dylan grabbed her arm.

Fatal mistake.

War rolled back his shoulders. His eyes locked on Dylan's hand. His fingers were wound way too tightly around Rose's fragile wrist. "Move it." That wrist was still faintly bruised from the cuffs.

Dylan focused only on her. "Forget him, Rose! We need to talk. That was some serious bullshit that went down last night. I-I didn't attack you. I didn't—"

"Get your damn hand *off* me," Rose told him.

When he didn't, she slammed her high heel down on his shoe.

*"What the hell? Rose—"*

War carefully pulled her out of his grip. "Excuse me." He eased her behind him.

"War?" Rose's finger poked at him.

Dylan the dumbass tried to get to her. "I can explain! I can tell you—" He grabbed for her again.

And that was it. War grabbed *him*. He caught the SOB's arm and twisted, yanking it up and high behind Dylan's back. Dylan let out a frantic yell— half pain, half horror. He tried to kick at War.

Stupid, weak kick.

War slammed the fool into the nearest wall.

"Security!"          Dylan          yelled. *"Suh...cure...it...eee!"*

Cordell assured him, "Don't worry. I'm calling the cops."

Dylan spun around and swung at War with a right hook. A pathetic hook. War dodged the blow and slammed back with his own fist. A direct hit to Dylan's nose that resulted in the crunch of bones and blood spurting down the man's face.

Dylan howled and his hands flew up to cover his nose.

War surged toward him. "You stay the fuck away from her."

"War...*enough*." Rose caught his arm and tugged him back.

Absolutely. He would let her tug him back. But if Dylan made any move toward her, if he tried to grab her again, War would stop the jackass.

"I want him arrested!" Dylan was pinching his nose. "When those cops get here, he should be arrested!"

Cordell moved to stand between them. His hands were on his hips.

A petite, elegantly dressed woman with perfectly styled short, black hair also stepped forward.

Simone Davis. The station manager. So she'd caught all the action, too? War opened his mouth—

"Brawling at the station. Unreported arrests. And after the way I've recently learned you treated Rose..." Simone shook her head. "You are fired. Clean out your desk."

Dylan dropped his bloody hand. "You can't do that!"

"Certainly, I can. It's my station! Rose is a star right now. She has an inside scoop on the biggest murder investigation in the city—"

Was that why Simone was kicking Dylan to the curb? Because she didn't want to lose her scoop? And not just because Dylan was a dick?

"And you are delusional if you think I will not do anything and everything to protect my station. You are *out*." She nodded to Cordell. "Make sure he packs up his desk."

Cordell grinned. "With pleasure!"

When Cordell closed in, Dylan threw up a hand. "No! No! I am filing assault charges—*against him*." He pointed to War. "You all saw it. You're witnesses! Whether you want to be or not...you saw it!" His gaze jumped to Rose. "You saw what this psycho did. You're honest, Rose. You tell the truth. One of the things I love about you."

Had he just used the *l*-word with her? War's hands fisted as a growl vibrated in his throat.

Rose's hold tightened on his arm. "Do not. I get what you were doing, but *stop*." Her voice was low.

"We all saw." It was Cordell who spoke. "I will happily give a statement about what I witnessed. First you..." He pointed at Dylan. "You hit War in the jaw. War didn't touch you before that. You swung first. Then you grabbed his girl. He was pulling her out of your way, putting her behind his back to keep her out of the range of your flying fists, and you went at him again. The man defended himself. You can't fight for shit, by the way, so you're lucky he didn't leave you in a bleeding heap on the floor."

An option that War considered to still be on the table.

"Same thing I saw," Simone informed them crisply. "You created a spectacle, Dylan. You are *done*."

His mouth was opening and closing, but Dylan couldn't seem to find words. Slowly, his gaze slid around the assembled group until his stare locked with War's.

Now, War did smile. "I think you might be the one with control issues, not me." Because he'd played the scene exactly the way he wanted. Dylan had attacked. He'd defended. Now Dylan would be the one... "Guess you'll be having another long sit-down with the cops, huh?" Dylan would be the one taken out of the picture. "Have fun with that."

A guttural yell burst from Dylan. He shoved Cordell as he surged toward War. Immediately, War pushed Rose to the side. *You will not hurt her.*

But as Dylan barreled past Rose—who was moving closer, not away—War saw her quickly sweep out her foot. She swept it right against Dylan's rushing legs.

Dylan went down in a shuddering crash.

"Guess you didn't hear the message the first time." Rose glared down at him. "You're fired."

# CHAPTER FOURTEEN

"You did it deliberately."

War reached for a shot glass and poured a quick drink into it before sliding it down the bar toward Rose. Monday night. Armageddon was always closed on Monday.

Dylan had been hauled away. Rose had finished up her day at the station—even stayed to film her anchor segment for the five o'clock news. She hadn't wanted to go home. He'd seen the tension pouring from her.

A stop by Armageddon had seemed like a good idea. They could grab a drink. Have some privacy. Then he could go upstairs to his new PI office and check some files for additional data about—

"You goaded Dylan into attacking you. That way, you could be the victim." Her fingers closed around the glass, but she didn't lift it to her lips. "I suppose you think that was sneaky?"

He filled his own shot glass. Saluted her. "Sneaky. Smart. A sonofabitch move. Whatever you want to call it." He swallowed down the shot. "He had it coming." That and a whole lot more.

"Do you always get revenge on those who...ah, have it coming?"

The glass tapped against the bar top. "Why don't you get to the real questions?"

Her head tilted.

"You heard everything he said to me."

"I did catch the highlights. Would have been hard to miss them."

"And now you want to know...are you sleeping with a killer?"

She shook her head.

"No? You don't want to know? Or maybe you already have the answer." He should have expected Gary to start digging in his past. Dylan was pulling out all the stops to get Rose away from War. *Like that shit doesn't make you look guilty as fuck, Dylan.* What he hadn't realized was just how quickly Gary would hit paydirt.

Too quickly. *Who have you been talking to, Gary?*

"I do have the answer already," Rose replied in a cool-as-you-please tone. "I'm not afraid of you. I don't think you have some addiction to danger or that you can't hold on to your control. I don't worry that you'll fly into some crazy fit and start attacking people around you." She stared straight into his eyes. "You've never been rough with me."

"I never *would* be."

Her gaze swept over his face. "You have more control than anyone I've ever met before."

Not always, he didn't. "Uh, you just saw me break your producer's nose."

"We both know you could have kicked his ass a dozen times by now."

True. He'd certainly been tempted.

"And you could have done a whole lot more damage than you did."

A shrug was his response. Again, though, she was right. With little effort, he could have made Dylan wind up in a body cast.

But that wasn't who he'd been raised to be. Wasn't the man who Odin's parents—and Odin— had helped him to be.

*Don't ever hit first.* That had been Odin's life advice to him. Good advice. Advice Odin's father had followed up with, *Make sure the enemy has it coming.*

And then...

*And make your blow count.*

Dylan was cooling his heels in jail. War figured that sure as shit counted.

"Did being a SEAL teach you that control?" She was still holding her glass. Not drinking from it.

"So...first rule of being a SEAL..." A wry smile curved his mouth. "Baby, you don't talk about it. Some guy comes in bragging about that life, then ten to one he never served on the team." As he stared at her, his smile slowly faded. "When I was serving, I learned that you do anything necessary to get the job done. You don't stop, no matter what. Pain. Fear. Rage. None of that can have a place in you. You focus on the mission, and you get it done."

"And right now...your mission is helping me to find the killer."

"Damn straight. I will do anything to get that job done."

"Is that why you pushed Dylan? You still think he might be guilty even though he was locked up when I got the call?"

"I pushed Dylan—one, because he was a prick who deserved to get pushed. He needs to work on *his* freaking control. And, two, I did it because, yeah, I'm suspicious as hell about him. I don't like his focus on you. I've handled some stalking cases while I've been in the area, and they can get ugly, fast. The stalkers are careful. They know how not to cross the line and get the cops involved. They know how to isolate their victims. Make them feel helpless. Out of options. Then those bastards close in..." He reached for a bottle. Stopped. "My second client when I moved here. She was a twenty-two-year-old woman who was being stalked. She needed proof to get a restraining order. I was getting her that proof. But while I was working on things, her stalker slipped into her house. He had a gun, and he planned to kill her."

"*War.*"

"Just so happened, I was coming by to update her on the progress of my investigation. I heard her scream." He'd never forget that terrified sound. "It was luck that I was there. Luck that kept her alive. I kicked in the door. Hauled him off her." He'd gotten nicked by a bullet that asshole had fired, but War didn't see the point in mentioning that. "Stalkers are dangerous. They escalate quickly. With Dylan having pictures of you, being so focused on you..." War shook his head. "I am not going to play with your safety. He needed to know that if he came at you, I'd be there to kick his ass." A ghost of a smile curved his lips.

"Now he also knows that *you* will kick his ass, too. That was one hell of a leg sweep, by the way."

"Thanks." She didn't smile back. "I had this boyfriend once who taught me the move. He kept insisting that I learn how to protect myself. Told me the world was a dangerous place and a woman should always have a few tricks up her sleeve."

"A boyfriend, huh? And he taught you that phenomenal move? He must have been a freaking prince."

She swallowed the liquid in her shot glass and pressed the glass back to the tabletop. "We broke up."

"Because he was an ass." His gaze didn't leave her. "A jealous, possessive, not-understanding-what-he-had ass."

"Sure, okay. I was gonna say we had trust issues, but that works, too."

War fought his smile. God, he fucking loved her. He—

*Holy. Shit.*

"Are you okay?" She leaned across the bar and slapped him on the back. "You look like you're choking."

He swallowed. Twice. Finally managed, "Do we...still have those issues?"

She slowly lowered back onto the bar stool. "I don't know. You tell me."

Another swallow. Then he was walking from behind the bar. His steps seemed extra loud in the silence around them. He made his way to her. She swiveled on the stool to face him. Her expression was intent. Watchful.

He knew this moment was important. His hands wanted to shake so he balled them into fists. The realization he'd just had—the one that had sent the earth trembling beneath his feet— still had him struggling to cope.

His emotions for Rose hadn't died after the breakup. Being with her again, if anything, what he felt for her was so much stronger now. Because it was stronger, he had to be careful. If he screwed up with her again, if she walked again, he'd be sent to hell.

Life without her *was* hell.

His voice was gravel-rough as he told her, "I would trust you with my life."

"That's an easy one," she surprised him by replying.

Easy? No way, no day, it was not.

"I trust you with my life, too. Always have. If I didn't still trust you to keep me safe, I would have hired a different bodyguard. Especially considering that bit of business you pulled by having a secret deal with the cops." Her gaze didn't leave his. "But I know—deep down—I *know* you would do everything you could to protect me if I was in danger. You'd probably even try to jump between me and a bullet."

He angled closer to her. "There is no 'probably' about it." He wanted her mouth. But first, they needed to get some business cleared up between them. "I would definitely jump between you and a bullet."

"Then I guess it's a good thing he's not firing bullets."

No, this bastard preferred a far more personal kill method. He wanted to touch his victims as he ended their lives. War had done some research on this particular brand of bastard while she'd been filming that day. What he'd learned about killers who choked their victims...

Strangulation murders often had a sexual component for the killers. They got off on choking their victims, stealing their breath, watching them struggle.

"Hey." Her hand rose and pressed to his cheek. "Where did you just go?"

His head turned. His lips feathered over her palm. "I wish I'd killed him. When I found him with you in that motel room, I wish that I had killed the bastard then."

"War..."

Another kiss. "You can trust me to keep you safe. I won't fail you again, Rose."

"I-I said I trusted you." Her voice had gone husky. Her eyes were so deep. He couldn't look away. Didn't want to look away.

"You trust me...with your life."

A nod.

"What about with your heart, baby? What do I have to do in order to get you to trust me with that again?"

She sucked in a startled breath.

"Because I will do it. Whatever it is. Know that whatever happens in the future, *I am on your side*. I believe you. I believe *in* you." He'd never trusted a lover that completely before. Never cared enough to risk so much. But this was Rose. She was different. He would be different with her.

"I give you my word. I will never doubt you. I will never hesitate where you are concerned."

"Why does...why does how I feel matter so much?"

"That's an easy one." He deliberately used her words. "Because you matter." If she didn't realize that, he'd screwed up again. "You are my priority. I will prove myself to you."

"You don't have to—"

"Yeah, I fucking do."

Now she was the one to swallow. "War..."

He waited. He was so close to her. He could feel the warmth of her body reaching out to him. Could smell her delicious scent. As he watched, her little pink tongue slid over the edge of her lower lip.

"Kiss me?" Rose asked. Voice husky. Sexy. Inviting.

His mouth pressed to hers. Open-mouthed. Hot. Hungry. The first kiss was tasting. Needing. Then he moved even closer. Kissed her harder. Deeper. Thrust his tongue past her lips and tasted her. She moaned, and he greedily drank in the sound. Her taste was incredible, and he just wanted more and more and more. He wanted *everything* he could get from her. He would always want everything. With Rose, there were no limits.

"Fuck me," she whispered against his mouth. *Kiss me. Fuck me.*

Oh, hell, yes, he would gladly oblige.

He pulled back, but just enough so that he could lift up her shirt and toss it on the bar top. Her breasts pressed against the dark blue cups of her bra, and he bent to brush his lips against her skin.

*"War!"*

He reached behind her. Undid the clasp of the bra, and soon her breasts were spilling into his hands. He loved her nipples. Loved how tight they'd get and the way she would shiver when he stroked them. And he was stroking...stroking and licking and driving her wild.

He loved her this way. Hungry. Hot. Wanting him so badly that—

"No way. Not...happening."

War stilled. His heart thundered.

"You're not doing this to me this time." Her breath heaved in and out as her hands pushed against him. "You're not going to make me go insane while you stay in control. This time, that control of yours is breaking."

"Uh, Rose..."

She jumped from the barstool. Stood before him in her pants and her heels with those perfect breasts thrusting ever-so-perkily toward him and making him nearly drool.

Her hand went to the front of his jeans. Her fingers stroked over the rock-hard length of him through the denim, and his eager dick jerked and twitched more for her.

"I want to see what it's like when you go over the edge." She undid the button. Eased down the zipper. Shoved his jeans out of her way. His cock sprang into her hands, and she stroked him— softly at first. Teasingly. Gently. Then her grip became firmer. Her strokes a little more demanding. And, of course, his dick loved every single thing she was doing to him. His legs had locked down. His whole body had gone tight with tension. He'd clamped his jaw shut and she was—

Lowering before him. Hitting her knees in Armageddon as her mouth moved toward his dick. He couldn't look away from the sight of her. *Nothing* in the entire world was as sexy as Rose going down on him. He was so turned on just by the image of her before him that a shudder worked the length of his body. He wanted to come. Wanted to explode right then and there, but he would *not*. He would hold onto his control. He would wait for her. His motto had always been ladies' first, and he wasn't going to—

Her lips closed around the tip of his cock. A guttural groan tore from him. "Now who is teasing?" he demanded.

She licked the head. "I'm just getting started." Her breath blew over him.

*His* breath panted in and out.

Then she opened her mouth wider. Took him in deeper.

No way could he stare at *his* woman, his Rose, on her knees, opening her mouth, and taking his cock inside and not lose his mind. With every lick of her tongue, every pull of her mouth on him, the fierce lust he felt for her roared inside of him. It grew stronger, hotter, fiercer with every second that passed.

His hands sank into her hair. Her beautiful hair. She was dipping toward him, her breasts were bobbing, her nipples tight, and her mouth...the sight of his dick sliding past her lips...

*"Rose."*

He was too close to the edge. His climax was building. He was going to come into her mouth. He was going to lose it—

She sucked harder. Deeper. Swirled her tongue over—

Something snapped inside of him. War felt it happen. Could seem to *hear* it.

In a blur, he pulled her up. Held her too tightly. Her lips were red and slick, her eyes shining. "So fucking beautiful." His voice was barely human. Too primal. With her in his arms, he rushed for the pool table.

"War?"

The way she said his name...the need...

She'd wanted him without control.

*Be careful what you wish for.*

He put her on the edge of the pool table. Tossed away her shoes and her pants, and pushed his cock at the entrance to her body. "Can't...go slow."

"I don't want slow. I want hard." Her nails sank into his shoulders. "I want uncontrolled. I want you..." Her mouth pressed to his neck. Lick. Bit. "Giving me everything that you've got."

He sank deep into her.

*"Just like that..."*

His right hand pushed between them. Rubbed her clit. War used fingers to drive her crazy even as his dick slid in and out. In and out. She was wet and tight, and his thrusts were frantic. There was no holding back. He couldn't have, even if he'd wanted to go slow.

Everything was too basic. Too desperate.

She surged up against him as a choked scream burst from her, and her inner muscles clamped even tighter around him. He knew she was coming.

He didn't slow down.

His hand pulled away from her clit. He hauled her closer to the edge of the pool table as his fingers curled around her waist. Her legs locked around him as he pistoned against her. A fury of need tore through him. War felt like he couldn't get close enough to her. Couldn't sink in deep enough. He wanted to mark her. Leave an impression on her very soul so that she knew, she *knew* that she was his.

Just as he was hers. She'd marked him from the beginning.

Her nails raked down his back. Her hips bucked against him. "War!"

She was coming a second time. Hell, yes. *Hell, yes*. The contractions of her delicate, inner muscles sent him straight into oblivion. His orgasm ripped through him as he drove deep into her once more. The release sucked his breath away, sent his heart pounding in a triple-time rhythm, and had every cell in his body burning with white-hot pleasure. There was no stopping as he jetted into her. There was no being easy. He was pumping his hips against her. Pressing his lips to the curve of her shoulder. Wrapping her in his scent. Taking her. Claiming her.

*Loving* her.

\*\*\*

"Well, hello, again." The detective put her hands on her hips as she studied Dylan. "Fancy seeing you here. But there are some people who just can't stay away."

"My lawyer will have me out of here in no time."

"Um." Her nose scrunched as she swept her gaze over his face. "That looks painful. But judging by the white tape, I'm assuming our lovely staff made sure you were patched up?"

He glared. This should *not* have happened. He'd made a mistake. Let that arrogant dick War drive him too far. He'd gone off script. Dylan knew better than to do that. He *never* went off script. "I need to talk to Rose."

Lynn Slater laughed. "You are hilarious."

He knew his rights. "I am entitled to one phone call! I want to call Rose!"

"You don't get to call the woman you've been stalking. That's not how things work."

"I am *not* stalking her! I told you, that evidence was planted. The photos were mine, but not the mask, not—" His eyes widened. "You know what? I bet *he* did it."

"He?" Lynn wasn't laughing any longer. Her hands were still on her hips.

"Warren—War—Channing! He wants me out of the way. He hates that I have a relationship with Rose."

"A relationship. Is that what you have?"

"We have a *working* relationship."

Lynn shook her head. "Not according to the station manager, you don't. She told one of my uniforms that you were not to set foot on that property again. That you'd been fired. Turns out, you didn't report those solicitation arrests to her."

Rage surged inside of him. "Did *you* tell War about that?"

"Why would I tell War something that is public knowledge? He's a PI. I'm sure he can dig up info like that easily enough." Her gaze raked him. "I'm sure he can dig up all kinds of things about you."

"You know I wasn't the one to call Rose last night! I was here with you!"

"And you're here with me again. Look at that."

His fists banged onto the table in front of him. "I want Rose!"

Her gaze flickered to his fisted hands. "Yes, that is abundantly apparent. But you know what else is apparent?" She strode toward him. Lightly skimmed her finger over the tape on his swollen nose. "You're not going to get what you want."

Because of War. Dylan *hated* him. "He's a killer. A liar. She has no clue what that man is really like."

"You know..." Her hand fell away as she propped one hip against the table. "If you really believe all of this about War, I'm surprised you keep screwing with him."

He—

Dylan frowned up at her.

"Because I'd think that if you push him too far, you'll get a whole lot more than a broken nose. I mean, if War *is* this cold-blooded, merciless killer...what do you think he'll do to you when you go after his lady again?"

A tendril of fear curled around Dylan's spine.

What would War do? He...he didn't think he wanted to find out.

# CHAPTER FIFTEEN

"Rose?" War pushed up and stared at Rose as she kind of flopped on the pool table.

*There's no 'kind of' about it.* She *was* flopping. Her heart still thundered far too loudly and quickly in her chest, and Rose was attempting to get her breath to go from frantic-pant level to normal.

"Are you okay?' He slid out of her.

She continued to flop, but her lips curled down as he withdrew. She'd rather enjoyed having him inside of her. When he was driving them both into oblivion, she didn't have to think about anything but pleasure.

She could already feel the real world trying to poke its way back into her brain.

"Did I hurt you?"

Her head moved in a slow, negative motion against the table. "Did I hurt you?" she returned.

He shook his head. She thought he might be lying. Rose was about ninety percent sure she'd left scratch marks down his back, but...maybe those hadn't hurt. She knew it took a lot to hurt big, bad War.

*A lot more than just me.*

She swallowed and sat up. "I need a shower." *Stat.* She eased off the pool table—*I'll never be able to look at it the same way again*—and hurriedly shimmied back into her panties. She caught her shirt and pulled it back on. She needed her bra, her pants—

But before she could grab the rest of her scattered clothing, War was wrapping his fingers around her wrist. "I have a shower you can use upstairs."

She automatically glanced up.

"Told you, I've been working on things up there. Got a PI office and a small apartment. You can shower off. Do anything you want."

What she wanted was a second round with War. But she knew they had things to do—or rather, one big thing. They had a killer to hunt.

War righted his own clothes—she hadn't even taken off his shirt, just shoved it out of her way—and scooped up the rest of her things. He led the way past a private door and up a narrow staircase. "There's an entrance outside the building, too," he explained. "But I wanted to be able to go back and forth from the bar." He unlocked a door near the top of the stairs and ushered her inside.

Her breath slid out in a slow whistle. "You've done an amazing job." He had. War enjoyed working with his hands. She knew that. He was, ah, very good with those hands.

The building was historic, like all the others along this block. He'd obviously spent a great deal of time restoring the second level. The hardwood floor gleamed. An antique chandelier hung overhead. A long, elegant couch waited to the right. There was another door there, one leading out...

Curious, Rose padded toward that door with its frosted glass. Her fingers curled around the knob, and she pulled the door open.

*Trouble For Hire, Private Investigations.* The words had been etched onto the frosted glass. "It's official, hmm?"

"Folks always said I was trouble. Guess the name stuck."

She could see a small lobby in the outer room. Another door—one that had several locks, all-bolted—and she suspected that door led outside.

"The bathroom is this way."

She shut the door. Turned back toward him. Stilled. His hair was tousled. His eyes had never seemed so dark—or so full of emotions. He wasn't staring at her like he wanted her. No, it was far, far more than that. He was staring at her like—

He glanced away. "Go down this hallway. Take a right. The bathroom is in there. You'll find some towels. Soap. Everything you should need."

She didn't go down the hallway. She found herself closing in on him. Rose wanted him to look at her again, the same way he'd just done. She *needed* him to do it—

"I was thinking...I know where we need to search next. Provided, of course, that you're up for another B&E."

His words had her doing a quick stumble.

"Dylan got his intel on me too quickly. I'm sure it was fed to him by Gary the Sleaze, and I want to know just when he got it. Just how long Dylan has been using his services."

"We're breaking into Gary's house?"

"We're swinging by his office." He waved a hand toward his own office. "A PI keeps the good intel locked away. I'm betting Gary has intel on Dylan."

"Maybe we should try going straight to Gary. Asking him for what he has. Instead of, you know, pulling another B&E." She took a few more steps toward him.

War's gaze dipped toward her. "Not loving the life of crime, huh?"

"It seems risky. Let's try Option A first. The option where we ask nicely."

His hand tucked a lock of hair behind her ear. "But, baby, I thought we covered that I didn't do nice so well."

She inhaled his crisp, masculine scent. "Something tells me that when you want to be nice, you can be. That you will do it amazingly well."

His hand lingered against her cheek. "Don't be so sure. I tried being the nice guy with you. Thought it gave me an in with you, but my true colors showed, and you couldn't get away fast enough." His hand started to drop.

She caught it. "You want me to trust you with my heart?"

A grim nod.

"Why?"

A half-smile curled his lips but didn't lighten his eyes. "Don't you know?"

"I'd like to have things clearly spelled out for me. That way, there is no confusion." No thinking she knew only to have her heart shattered again.

"I want you to trust me with it...because you fucking own *my* heart."

She shook her head. An instinctive move because he could not have meant—

"You own my heart. It's been yours the whole time. You just have to decide what you want to do with it."

For a moment, she couldn't move at all. "You, um, that's kind of a poetic thing to say."

"And I'm not a real poetic guy."

"That's not what I meant—"

"I know what I am. I'm the bastard who gets shit done. The one not afraid to play dirty. To *do* the dirty deeds that are necessary. I don't usually have pretty words. I don't say the *right* words. I screw up shit and that's just life." His lips thinned. "But I want to be different with you. You *make* me different."

Her breath sawed out. What he was telling her...the way he was looking at her again...

"You matter to me," he said simply. "Us being together—it always mattered to me."

"You were furious with me. When you came to find me at Finch's, you were ready to turn me over to the cops."

"You were in trouble. I was ready to do anything to keep you safe. Even shit that made you mad, like working with the cops." No hesitation. No BS. "I'd still do anything. A little B&E barely blips on my radar. I don't mind breaking the law for you. I don't mind lying. Hell, sweetheart, if it meant that you stayed safe, I'd kill for you in a heartbeat."

She took a quick step back. "No. I don't want that. I never want that."

"Does it scare you? Who I really am, deep inside? Because I don't want you scared. But I also don't want you mistaking me for someone else."

Uh, yeah, that was an impossible task. There was no one else like War.

"You wanted me to lose control."

And he had and the sex had been phenomenal. So good that she could still feel little aftershocks of pleasure inside even as they had this insane conversation.

"Losing control during sex means we both go wild."

They had.

"Losing control out of the bedroom..." A muscle flexed along his hard jaw. "That can't happen. I was trained to be dangerous. I *am* dangerous. I was good at my missions. When Dylan was spouting his mouth about me liking adrenaline, he wasn't wrong. The rush is as natural to me as breathing. The dark parts of life call to me. I know how evil people can be. I know that sometimes, you have to go to extreme lengths to stop that evil." His gaze swept over her face. "I don't want you to see me pushing extremes. There will be no limits in the bedroom, but outside of it, I *have* to keep that control. I need it. People around me need it."

"You..." She stopped. Gathered her thoughts. "I think you're revealing more to me now than you did the entire time when we used to be together."

"That's because if I said too much about myself before, I was afraid of scaring you off."

Did it appear that she was running away? "I'm not scared."

"No, you don't look like you are." His gaze dipped to her mouth. "I'm not making the same mistakes this time," he growled.

"Neither am I."

His hands reached for her, but—

His phone rang. A loud, heavy metal sounding blast. He'd tossed the phone on his desk when he came into the office. As the phone blasted again and vibrated, War swore. He backed away and scooped up the device. He quickly put the phone to his ear. "Odin, your timing could not be worse..."

Actually, Rose thought it could have been worse. Odin could have called when they'd been, ah, playing a game of pool.

"What?" War barked.

Her spine straightened.

"The SOB was sniffing around my place?"

Which SOB? She inched closer.

"Damn straight I want you to hold him. Rose and I will be right there." He ended the call. His fingers remained tight around the phone. "Remember that plan about me playing nicely with good old Gary?"

Cautiously, she nodded. It had been a very recent plan. Not like she could have forgotten it already.

"Consider the plan altered. Odin just found that jackass slinking around my beach cabin. He's spying on me, and I want to know why." His eyes glittered. "How fast can you make that shower?"

"Give me two minutes."

"Done."

***

Odin tossed his phone onto the couch. "Get comfortable." He waved toward the PI. "You're not going anywhere."

The jerk immediately jumped to his feet. As if Odin had not just said...*get comfortable.* "You can't keep me here!" Gary Strom blasted. "There is no way you can make me stay!"

Odin looked at Gary, then glanced down at his own body. No way, huh? He outweighed the man by one whole hell of a lot. Bigger, stronger, meaner...Gary did not want to play this game. Odin crossed his arms over his chest. "Want to bet?"

Gary gulped.

*Yeah, that's what I thought.* Some people were all about picking on those who were smaller and weaker.

Odin had always hated those kinds of people.

# CHAPTER SIXTEEN

"Gary, Gary, Gary..." War cocked his head to the left. "Do you have any idea how badly you screwed up a perfectly good night?"

"You can't keep me here!" Gary snapped.

From his position near the window, Odin frowned over at Gary. "He keeps saying that. It's like he doesn't even know who we are."

"Oh, I think he has a very good idea of who we are." Too good of an idea. "Didn't I warn you to stay away?"

Gary swallowed. His gaze darted around the room, as if looking for help. The dude was not going to find it. Odin appeared pissed as hell—the exact same way that War felt. Rose was staring suspiciously at the PI from her perch in War's favorite, over-stuffed chair.

Gary's gaze dipped on them all, then slid past the frame that sat on War's end table. Odin must have been tidying—the guy was a serious neat freak—because the frame was now sitting up again. Gary barely looked at the frame before his stare zoomed around as if searching for—

"Help is not going to magically appear," War informed him. "So how about we cut to the chase?

And by that, I mean, why the fuck are you hiding outside of my home?"

"I wasn't hiding!" Gary instantly denied as his gaze shot back to War. "I was...doing recon work. You know the business. You know how it is."

Oh, he knew the business, all right. "I know I told you to keep your ass away. I know you didn't listen." He took an aggressive step toward Gary. "I know that pisses me off."

Sweat dotted Gary's wide forehead. "He offered me double, okay?"

"Dylan?"

A jerky nod. "Offered me double my usual pay to find some shit on you that he could use. He, um, doesn't like for you to be around her." A vague motion of his hand toward Rose.

Rage burned inside of War. "Too fucking bad. Around her happens to be my favorite place." Around her. *In* her. No one was going to keep him away.

Not ever again.

Gary raked a hand through his already disheveled hair. "I gave him all the intel I had on you."

Voice silky as he took yet another step toward his prey, War asked, "And what intel would that be?"

Gary risked a glance at Odin. Then back to War. "About the stuff you've done as a SEAL. About all those black ops missions."

Curiosity pulled at War. "Just how would you get access to classified intel?"

Gary's pointed chin lifted. "I'm a better PI than you think."

*I highly doubt that.* "You just got caught outside of my place. If you were good, Odin wouldn't have seen you."

Gary shrugged.

"What did you *think* you would find on me by hiding outside?"

Gary hunched his shoulders but didn't speak. Annoying.

"Gary? I'm getting bored," War prompted.

"Thought you'd be screwing someone else," Gary finally snapped. "I could get a pic and give that to Dylan. Double pay. Easy money."

Rose had been silently watching, but at those words, she surged to her feet. "You are such an ass!"

Gary flinched.

"Stop trying to ruin people's lives! Try doing some real work. Find missing people. Track down criminals. Recover stolen property!" Red burned in her cheeks. "Don't try to destroy people that you don't know." She rushed toward Gary with blood in her eyes.

War wrapped his arm around her shoulders and pulled her to his side before she could attack. "Easy."

"I do not feel like being easy!"

Fair enough. He bent his mouth to her ear. "Guess you don't want to be nice anymore?"

Her answer was a snarl.

God, she was wonderful.

Keeping his arm around her shoulders and keeping Rose close to him, War lifted his head and peered at Gary. "She doesn't want to be nice."

"Uh..." Gary's sweat situation was getting worse.

"If she doesn't want to be nice, that means I don't have to be nice, either. The way I see it, you're an intruder."

"What? No, no, I'm—"

"You were trying to get into my home. When my buddy Odin and I caught you, we had to use force to stop you."

"Oh, shit," Gary whispered as his eyes widened. "Shit."

War eased his arm from around Rose and closed the final bit of distance between him and Gary. His head tilted to the left. "That will be the explanation I think we'll give to the cops." He nodded. His head slid to cock on the right. "I like that plan. Let's get this show moving—"

"*Wait!*" Rose's voice. She'd just grabbed his arm. "Before things get uncomfortably physical for Gary, give him a minute to talk."

"Oh, shit," Gary said again.

"He's not saying anything helpful," War noted.

She pushed War to the side so she could glare down at Gary. "That's about to change, isn't it, Gary? Because if it doesn't, I don't think you will like what happens next."

War would not smile at her. But, damn, the woman was doing an impressive rendition of good cop, bad cop.

Gary swallowed a few times, then he blurted, "It wasn't him."

"Who are we talking about?" War wanted to know. The PI was trying what little patience he had.

"Dylan. It wasn't him."

"Gary..." Rose sighed out the name. "If you want me to keep War from attacking, you'll have to give me information that actually makes sense."

Gary bobbed his head. "I know you're working on those strangulation cases. You think it was Dylan. But it wasn't him. That woman—that time in Tampa? The night she was killed? He was with me. I can alibi him."

Now this was new information. "Why were you working with him in Tampa?"

"I was supposed to dig up some info on a local politician. Catch him with his pants down and all that jazz." A click of his Adam's apple as Gary swallowed again. "Dylan and I got to drinking and talking, and then the next day, we heard the news about that woman. I'm telling you, Dylan didn't do it. He's not some serial killer or whatever the hell you suspect he is. The guy might not be a prince charming type—"

"Oh, you think?" Rose cut in.

"But he's not a killer. You can move him off your list."

"I got a call from the perp while Dylan *was* in jail," Rose said crisply. "So, yes, we'd already realized that unless he was working with someone else, Dylan wasn't the perp we were after."

Gary's eyes gleamed. "So you *are* still looking for the perp."

Yes, they were. They wouldn't stop looking until they had the guy caged behind bars. "Do you have something we need to know about him?"

Gary hesitated.

War grabbed the guy by the shirtfront and hauled him up. *"You have something we need to know?"*

"I-I can tell you...my fee is normally a grand to do—"

*"Someone tried to kill Rose, and you are charging me a fucking fee for the intel?"* He yanked Gary away from the chair and shoved him against the nearest wall. Hard. "You don't want to play with me right now. You want to tell me exactly what you—"

"Her informant!"

War stilled. His fist might have been heading straight for Gary, but it stopped, hovering about two inches away from its target.

"You know he's already out of jail? Made some deal and was walking out of the doors of the station almost as fast as he was walking in."

No, War had not been aware of that fact about Billy. He glanced to the side and saw that Odin had silently stepped forward.

Rose eased closer, too.

"I-I saw him when I was tailing her a few times."

"Billy meets with me often," Rose said with a roll of her shoulders. "He provides me information that I can use in my reports."

Gary glanced over at her. "No, this wasn't about meeting with you. You didn't know he was there. He was watching you."

Rose was at War's side. His fist had released and his hand had fallen down. She studied Gary a moment, then shook her head. "No. I don't believe you."

He gaped at her. "Why the hell not?"

"Because you're a sleazy guy who has lied to me before. Because while Billy may have experienced trouble with the law—"

War sent her a fast glance. Was that what she wanted to call it?

"I have never known of him to be violent toward anyone," Rose finished.

Was the woman forgetting that Billy had come at War with a knife?

As if remembering, she gave a little wince and a side-eye glance toward War. "He was scared that time."

*Uh, huh.*

Her gaze shifted back to Gary. "Billy knew where I was practically the entire time I went off-grid, so if he wanted to kill me, he could have done it."

Billy had known about her motel room. The room where she'd been attacked. "Ah, Rose..." War began.

"If you have proof about Billy, I want to see it."

That sounded fair. War crossed his arms over his chest. "Show her the proof," he ordered Gary.

Odin grunted. He obviously liked the plan, too.

"I don't have it on me!" Gary exclaimed. "You'll have to come with me to my office to get it."

Wasn't that convenient?

"I can show you everything." A desperate promise. "Just come with me." He exhaled. "And if you think I deserve a payment for what I show you…"

War didn't think Gary deserved a payment for anything. "I'll come to your office. You'll show me everything." He backed up. "Get your ass in your car. I'll be right behind you."

Gary rushed out.

Rose tapped his arm. "Excuse me. I think you made a mistake."

War turned toward her.

"What you meant to say was that *we* would be right behind him."

Grimly, he shook his head.

"Another mistake," Rose informed him crisply. "You meant to nod."

Gary was gone. War could hear the sound of a revving engine outside, rising above the thunder of the waves. "I don't trust the bastard, either."

"Yes, that makes two of us—"

"Three," from Odin.

Her luscious lips thinned. "The fact that *none* of us trust him means that one person doesn't go face-off with him alone."

"The fact that we don't trust him means that you need to stay damn far away from the bastard," he retorted.

Frustration darkened her expression. "*War…*"

"Please."

A furrow appeared between her brows. "Do you think if you say 'please' to me in that low, sexy voice, then I will just magically jump and do what you want?"

A guy could dream. "I'm worried it's a trap."

She blinked.

"I don't trust him. He is far too tight with Dylan, and it's pretty obvious that Gary will do anything for money."

"No denying that," Odin agreed.

"For all we know, he's trying to lure you to his office. I can't risk that." No, it was more... "I can't risk *you.*"

Rose huffed out an angry breath. "You're going to leave me behind? What in the hell is to stop me from just going after you?"

He jerked his thumb toward Odin. "I'm thinking he will."

Odin smiled at her. "Hi."

She growled. "Do not pull this testosterone bullshit."

"It's not bullshit." It wasn't. He wasn't playing some macho game. "It's me wanting to make certain that the person who matters most to me is protected."

"What about me wanting to protect *you*?" Rose surged toward him. "Did you think of that? Did you stop to think that, you know, maybe Rose might be worried about me?"

Her being worried—he saw that as a good sign. She had to care in order to worry.

"I can handle myself," War assured her. "You hired me because I was a tough bastard, remember?"

"You aren't even letting me pay you anything! We never discussed payment!"

That was because there was no way he was going to let her pay him. His protection was free for Rose. He would do anything for her. Always.

"And you were supposed to help me catch the killer. That was the whole point of our partnership!"

War nodded and angled his head to the right. "Exactly."

Horror flashed on her face. "Oh, no!"

Oh, no...what?

"You're doing your game-on thing. Like you've already reached a conclusion."

Odin cleared his throat. "Gary is gone. Might want to speed this scene along."

"I have reached a conclusion. I'm going to keep up my side of the partnership. I'm checking out Gary's so-called evidence. I'm also keeping *you* safe. Odin will make sure that nothing happens to you."

Her hands curled around War's shoulders. "This plan sucks."

His head lowered so that his forehead could press to hers. "I need you safe."

"I need you the same way! Look, why not at least take Odin with you? That way, you have him watching your back—"

"I have Odin watching what matters most." He needed to go. "Don't worry. I can handle Gary—and anything he throws at me."

"Such confidence." Her hands tightened on him. "You'd better not be wrong," she muttered. "You come back to me with so much as a scratch, and I will be exceedingly pissed off."

He eased back from her. "I'll be back before you can even miss me." War headed for the door.

"Well, that's a bunch of bullshit." Her disgruntled voice followed him. "I've been missing you for weeks."

His shoulders stiffened. "It's like I've been living with a hole where my heart was."

"War?"

He glanced back. "You won't have to miss me. I'm coming back. An hour, two tops. I've got this." Then he left because he *needed* to keep her safe. And if she kept looking at him with those big, gorgeous eyes...

No. His willpower would not falter. Odin would keep watch over her. War would deal with the PI. And if it turned out that Billy *had* been keeping secrets...

Then maybe they'd be solving this case, and Rose could get her full life back again—and a killer would be off the streets.

\*\*\*

"Well, that sucked." Rose glared at the closed door. *It's like I've been living with a hole where my heart was.*

"His intentions are good."

The waves pounded against the shore. "His intentions are shit." She took a step forward.

Odin blocked her path. "Hello, again."

"Don't be cute."

His smile stretched a little more.

"Aren't you worried about him? We don't know what War is facing."

"He's facing a squirrelly PI that War could handle in his sleep. He has this. But if he thinks that you could be in danger, the man's focus will be off. We don't want that."

Oh. Someone was being chatty. And making a point. She knew that War could easily handle Gary, it was just that— "He cut me out of my investigation."

"That's not what's making you so upset."

"Now you're analyzing me?"

"You know War will bring you anything he finds."

Yes, fine, she did know that. Still—

"You don't want him hurt. You want to protect him. Even though he's trained to fight and defend himself in dozens of ways, you still have this urge to protect him." He sounded a little...surprised. "It's sweet."

"Sweet," she gritted in disgust. "There is not enough cookie dough ice cream in the world for me to deal with you, but I am still going to see what I can find." With that, Rose whirled on her heel and stalked for the kitchen.

"Ah...what are you doing?" He trailed behind her.

"Stopping myself from chasing after War." Because she did know that he could handle this, it was just—

*I want to be at his side. I do want to look out for him, and I don't care how much training he has.* She did worry, dammit. But she also got— intellectually—that he had this scene. He could take care of things. And, yes, sure, on the off chance that it was some kind of setup...

Her staying put was a sound choice. She didn't like that choice, but she was dealing with it in her way. Rose yanked open the freezer. Her breath expelled in a relieved rush when she saw that he still had her favorite ice cream flavor waiting inside. She grabbed the container.

"Um, Rose—"

She put the ice cream on the counter and grabbed for the utensil drawer. "It's called stress eating. I do it. Don't be judgy. It's also called...I haven't eaten all day and I need something so I don't get shaky and crazy and—" She'd opened the drawer. Shoved her hand inside to snag a spoon.

Except she wasn't staring down at a spoon. Spoons were there. Knives. Forks. Plus, something else. Something awfully shiny. "What is *that*?"

Odin's big hand flew into the drawer. He pulled out two spoons. "One for you. One for me." He shoved the drawer shut.

Too late.

She ignored the offered spoons and hauled the drawer right back open again. The glinting diamond ring was still there, nestled in the empty spot next to the spoons. "Why is there a ring in War's utensil drawer?"

Odin cleared his throat. "You should ask War about that. Have a spoon." He dangled it before her and used his hip to shut the drawer.

She swatted the spoon out of the way. "War's not here. He left so I can't exactly ask him why a diamond ring is shining in his drawer. But I am asking you. Seeing as how you are his BFF and all, I thought you'd know."

He shrugged.

"Odin. You know."

He reached for the ice cream container. Dipped his spoon inside. "I know...that you should talk to him."

She yanked open the drawer again. "Is there someone else?" she asked, voice cracking.

"What? Hell, no. He can't even see anyone but you."

Her hand pressed to her chest. She couldn't look away from the ring.

"Ice cream is melting over here. Waste of some good cookie dough."

Slowly, she shut the drawer. "Who hides a ring like that in a drawer?"

"Same damn question I had. Drip. Drip. Drip. Still melting."

Rose glanced over at him.

His words had been light, but when she met his gaze, she saw that his bright stare was flat. Hard.

"War has been abandoned by a lot of people in his life," Odin said.

She took one of the spoons. Didn't dip it into the ice cream.

"Trusting isn't easy for him. In fact, trust is pretty much the hardest thing in the world for him. When people let you down over and over again, you start to expect the worst. He screwed up with you. He knew it as soon as you walked out of the door, but he thought you'd moved on. And, deep down, I think War believes that since so many people have left—his parents, all the fucking relatives who wouldn't take in an innocent kid, friends in battle who sold out his team—"

Her breath caught.

"After all that, it's hard not to think that maybe something is wrong with *you*." He sampled some ice cream. All casual-like. "Ever wonder why he works so hard to keep that control of his in place?"

Only every single day.

"It's because he thinks if he lets it crack, people won't like what he has inside. Personally, I like War just as he is. Arrogant bastard. Sneaky PI. Growling bar owner. True-as-hell friend."

She pulled the ice cream from Odin. "I happen to like him just fine that way, too."

Odin's harsh expression relaxed. "That's good to know."

# CHAPTER SEVENTEEN

"Show me the evidence," War demanded as he stalked into Gary's office. Gary's PI business was located in a nest of office spaces on a narrow, two-lane road. The building was brown and flat, and the sign outside of Gary's business had faded over time. *Strom Securities and Investigation.*

Gary glanced up as he turned on a lamp that sat on his desk. "Where's Rose?"

*Safe.* "She stayed with Odin. No sense wasting her time if you don't have the real deal for me."

Gary's lips pursed. "I do think we should cover my fee before I show you what I have."

*You're an asshat.* "I think you should show me what you have before I lose what little patience I have remaining."

He sniffed. "You're kind of like a bull, aren't you? Charging at everything in your line of sight."

"Gary, when I charge at you, you'll know it." He kept his arms loose at his sides.

"Don't shoot the messenger," Gary mumbled. He moved to the side and slid a key into the lock on his tall filing cabinet. The cabinet drawer let out a loud screech as he pulled it open, and then Gary snagged a manila file. He stared down at the file and slowly exhaled. "I wasn't one hundred percent honest with you."

"I am shocked." Not even a little bit.

Gary peered up at him. "I *did* see Billy tailing her. But I wasn't supposed to be getting pics of him, so I didn't worry about the guy. I focused on my target."

"You focused on Rose."

"Um." He gripped the file too tightly. "Since you came without her, this probably will work out better."

War's stomach twisted. "What's in the damn file?"

Gary dropped the file onto his desk. "Why don't you see for yourself?"

That twisting in his stomach got worse. He didn't like Gary's satisfied tone. The guy's eyes were all gleamy. *Like a cat that ate a big-ass canary*. War strode forward and flipped open the file. And he saw—

"She's not the perfect princess. But I figured you knew that after you got the first photo."

War's fingers shoved through the pictures before him.

"What I don't get...why did you take her back? Did she say that she'd changed? Because she hasn't."

The photos were all of Rose.

Rose. Rose dancing with some blond asshole. Rose kissing him.

Rose with her arms wrapped around a dark-haired bastard. The man was pressing his mouth to her throat.

Rose...slipping off her shirt as some guy stood—

Carefully, War slid the pictures back inside the file. He shut the file. Tapped his fingers on top of it.

"Maybe you don't feel like protecting her any longer," Gary said, oozing sympathy. "Maybe you want to tell that bitch to hit the road—"

"Don't call her a bitch. *Ever.*" His fingers stopped tapping. His head tilted to the left. "Gary, why do you have a death wish?"

"What?"

"You bring me to this piss-hole of an office under false pretenses and then you show me your bullshit pictures?" Rage burned, but his control was in place. Locked down tight.

"They're not bullshit! I took those pictures of Rose—hell, one of them was taken just last week. Not like she's been sitting at home being bored like your sad ass—"

He lunged for Gary.

And Gary—that sonofabitch—swung a freaking gun up at him.

*Are you shitting me right now?* War grabbed Gary's wrist and slammed it back into the filing cabinet. He kept slamming it even as Gary howled, but War didn't stop, not until the gun hit the floor.

"Not loaded!" Gary screamed. "It was not freaking loaded! I was just trying to stop you from—"

War drove his fist into Gary's jaw. Gary's head flew back. The SOB must have a glass jaw because his eyes rolled back, and his body slumped.

War let him fall. Then he bent and picked up the gun. Checked it. "Want kind of idiot points an empty gun at someone?"

Gary let out a long, ragged groan.

"Answer me!"

Gary blinked groggily. His hand rose and slid along the edge of his face. "You broke my jaw."

"No, I didn't. But I am tempted as hell." He put the gun on the desk and hauled Gary to his feet. "What kind of game are you playing?"

Tears—real damn tears—filled Gary's eyes. "He said...d-double if you broke up with her!"

"Dylan? This is still all about that jerk?"

"The p-pictures..."

"Are fake. Your photoshop skills suck."

"They do not!"

"When Rose is kissing someone, that is sure as hell not what her expression is like. FYI, she also has a crescent-shaped birthmark on her right shoulder. The woman in your pic who was dropping her shirt was magically missing that mark."

Gary's lips shook. His whole body shook.

"I'm going to ask you some questions, Gary. You're going to answer them honestly. Depending on how satisfied I am with your answers, I may or may not beat the ever-loving-hell out of you." Ice cold. Each word bit from his mouth. His whole body was like ice, trapping the fire inside. The rage that had exploded because this asshat had tried to get him to turn on Rose. That he'd tried to pull them apart.

"L-let me go..." Gary whimpered.

"Hell, no. Question one. Did you ever see Billy tailing Rose?"

A rough shake of Gary's head. His red hair stuck to his sweaty forehead.

"A yes or no answer, Gary. I want to be clear."

"N-no."

"Wonderful." War drove his fist into Gary's face. Blood spurted from his lips.

"Ow!" Another howl. "What the hell was that for?"

"It's because you lied to me back at my place. I don't like lies. You deal straight with me, and I won't make you bleed again."

Gary swiped the back of his palm over his bleeding mouth. "You're...a f-freaking bastard, you know that? What...you get off on pain?"

"How about you worry a little less about what gets me off...and little more about how you're going to get through the next five minutes with me?"

Gary's breath heaved in and out as the blood dripped from his lips.

"Question two. Can you really alibi Dylan for the murder in Tampa?"

"Y...yes..." Gary squeezed his eyes shut and flinched, as if in preparation for a blow.

War's brows rose.

Slowly, Gary opened his eyes. "You—you didn't hit me."

*No shit.* "Question three. What was the point of those fake photos?"

"For you to leave her." Now he was speaking quickly. "Business has been slow, and I—he said *double* pay. He wanted me to find something to break you up. I told him about your past, but that didn't work. This was the next option."

"It was a screw-up of an option. I trust Rose. Fool me once, then I'm a fucking prick. Fool me twice..." His jaw locked. "And I will make you wish you'd never been born."

"Oh, God."

"You came at me with a gun, Gary."

"Unloaded! I hate guns! Can't st-stand them!"

"You lied about my girl."

"Sorry?"

"I'm hunting a killer, and you are wasting my time. I don't appreciate having my time wasted."

A lick of fire appeared in Gary's eyes. War knew the fool was going to attack even before Gary's chin notched up and he snarled, "Yes, well, I don't appreciate you *punching* me!" With that bold declaration, Gary swung at him.

The blow barely scraped War's shoulder.

In return, War drove his fist into Gary's stomach. All of the air heaved from the PI. "Good talk, Gary," War snapped. "Real good talk." The rage was getting too close to breaking through his control. War stepped back. He was done with Gary. He turned away. Moved around that big filing cabinet.

*"You cocky sonofabitch!"*

War glanced back. Gary was heaving the whole freaking filing cabinet at him. War's fist flew out and slammed into the side before it could crash into him. "Bad move, Gary." The rage cracked through the ice that had surrounded him. "Now you've pissed me off."

*\*\**

She was standing on the porch waiting for him. Odin had been swinging in the hammock. Not talking much because...*Odin*. But keeping her company and keeping a close watch on the property.

War approached slowly and climbed the stairs that led up from the beach. She could see the tension that was cloaking him, and nerves had her arms curling around her own stomach.

"See? He's still in one piece." Odin's unconcerned voice.

War opened the screen door. Stopped short when he saw her. A lot of emotions flashed on his face. Longing. Need. Pain. Anger.

"What happened?" Rose asked.

"Not secure out here." The gruff words were aimed at Odin. "Didn't you think you should keep her *inside*?"

"I consider the porch to be inside. It's a screened-in porch. Besides, I had an eye on her."

War's jaw tightened as he focused on Rose. "Billy wasn't tailing you. That was just a lie. Gary is still working for Dylan."

Relief swept through her because she *had* trusted Billy, and she hadn't wanted to be wrong about him. Her gaze darted over War, and a quick gasp came from her. "Your knuckles!"

He looked down.

"What happened?" She hurried to him and reached for his hand. Hadn't she told the man not to return with so much as a scratch? Rose thought she'd been exceedingly clear.

"Gary decided to try dumping a filing cabinet on me. See, he didn't like the way I responded when he pulled a gun on me. The idiot thought he'd retaliate. No big deal."

Her mouth dropped open. "That...that is a seriously big deal." She whirled and, keeping her grip on him, tugged him after her. "I'm cleaning your wounds."

"Hardly wounds. Some scratches. I was walking away. Gary grabbed the cabinet and shoved it down on me. My fist hit the metal."

Her shoulders tightened "And did your fist hit *him*?"

"More than a few times."

She led him to the sink. Turned on the water. Carefully washed his scraped knuckles.

"I was feeling pretty pissed," War allowed. "But all in all, I'd say I was doing a fairly decent job of holding back. Things didn't get really physical until he pulled the gun."

Her hand jerked on his.

"Not loaded. Gary said he didn't like using guns. I think he had the weapon as some kind of scare tactic. Like the sight of it was supposed to make me back down." A pause. "Obviously, I didn't back down."

"No." Fear squeezed her heart. What if the gun had been loaded?

"He set me off deliberately. He wanted me to attack."

She grabbed a cloth. Patted his fingers dry.

"How did he set you off?" Odin asked.

Rose gave a little jump of surprise. She hadn't heard Odin follow them inside.

"He had some bullshit pictures of Rose with other men. Dylan wanted him to do anything possible to break me and Rose up, so the jerk thought flashing those pics would send me over the edge."

Her head turned. She met War's eyes. "Pictures? Of me?"

"Knew they were fake. Like I said before...I will *always* trust you. You told me there hadn't been anyone since us. I believed you. Damn well didn't believe him."

The tension built between them as she gazed into his eyes. Those deep, dark eyes. "I should have gone with you."

His expression hardened. "Rose, it was all a setup. He didn't have intel for us. It was—"

"That way, I could have been the one with the bruised knuckles because if he'd flashed those fake photos with me there, I would have charged at him." Gary was a problem that needed to be eliminated.

War's stare seemed to heat as he stared at her.

She backed up and her hip bumped against the open drawer. The *slightly* open drawer. His utensil drawer.

Automatically, War's gaze dipped to the drawer. She saw his eyes widen. A flash of surprise.

"Yeah, I think it's my cue to leave. You've obviously got surveillance on Rose covered for the rest of the night." Odin's voice seemed overly loud. "I will just see myself out. No, no, really, I got this. Don't trip over yourselves helping me. I think it will probably be a good idea for me to spend the night at the apartment over the bar."

"Odin," War said.

"Yeah?"

"You're talking a lot. You do that when you've got a secret." His head swiveled toward Odin. "She found it?"

A nod from Odin.

"Right." A muscle flexed along War's jaw. "Night, Odin."

Odin threw up a hand in a quick wave as he strode away.

War reached around Rose. She did a little shimmy to give him more room. He fully opened the drawer. Only—the ring wasn't there.

Alarm flared in his expression.

Her fingers slid into her back pocket. She'd changed into jeans while she waited for him to return. She wiggled her fingers in the pocket and then lifted the ring. "Are you looking for this?"

# CHAPTER EIGHTEEN

He looked at the ring. Then at her face. "I can explain."

"You can? That would be great. I'd love to hear what you have to say."

*Okay. Do this.* "I love you, and I want to marry you. I knew it pretty much right after meeting you so...yeah. I had the ring. I was waiting for the right moment." No sense telling her he'd planned for that *moment* to be the night everything had gone to hell. No sense mentioning he'd had a catered meal waiting. Candlelight. The whole deal. Or that the next day, when he'd gone after her, he'd had the ring with him then, too. But he'd seen the flowers on her desk. Rose hadn't been there and—

They'd stayed apart.

*But I kept the ring.* Just as he'd kept on loving her.

"What did you say?" Rose's voice had gone hoarse. Her eyes were huge. Her hand fisted around the ring.

"I love you."

"We broke up."

He'd been in hell every single day without her. "And we're back together."

"You—you    think—you—"    Her    words
sputtered to a stop.

"I thought it might be too soon before, and I
was definitely fucking afraid it was too soon this
time, too. That's why the ring was hidden."

"Your kitchen drawer is not a good hiding
spot!"

"So Odin tells me..." He turned his palm
toward her. "I'll keep it some place safe."

She didn't give him the ring. "You said you
loved me."

A nod.

"Why would you say that?"

His head cocked. "Because it's true?"

Red bloomed in her cheeks. "You never said
you loved me before! It was just sex. Hot, intense,
crazy sex and—"

Fantastic sex, yes, but... "I tend to be
controlled about most things in my life."

"I noticed. Talked to Odin about that very
thing earlier. And I get it."

Odin was being way chatty now. He must like
Rose.

"I get that you need your control. I get that
trust is hard. But War, with me, you can let down
your guard. I don't want to hurt you. I've never
wanted that."

"I *am* different with you, Rose. I've always
been different with you. Controlled is the last
thing I am when it comes to you." That was why
he wanted to destroy every threat to her. "From
the first, I knew I was falling fast and hard. Your
smile would light me up, and I wanted to put the
world at your feet."

"You didn't say anything like that to me!"

"When something is important, you try not to screw it up." He'd tried to keep all of the ugly parts of his life from her. He'd thought he was protecting her, but now he saw he'd been putting up a wall that had kept her away. "I still managed to screw things up, so I figured this time, I'd try a different tactic."

"Tactic?"

"In battle, you learn that if one technique isn't working, you switch things up."

"We aren't battling."

He was. He was in the most important fight of his life. "I held back my feelings before. I held back far too much. The result was that I lost you. I won't hold back again, and I don't want you holding back, either. This time, I'm telling you everything." And the big everything was... "I love you, Rose."

She blinked rapidly.

Oh, no, were those tears in her eyes? "You don't have to say it back," he told her. "You don't have to feel it back. You don't need to do anything but...let's just keep going as we are. Let's see what happens. There is no pressure—" He went to take the ring.

She snatched it out of reach. "That belongs to me."

*And I want you to belong to me. Always.* "You have my ring, sweetheart. What can I do to have you?"

A tear leaked down her cheek and absolutely broke his heart. "War, I will—"

His phone was ringing. No way was he answering it. "Fuck it," War said. He kept his gaze locked on her. *This* mattered. She mattered.

The phone kept ringing. He didn't recognize the ringtone. Right then, he didn't care who was calling.

Rose mattered.

A faint line appeared between her eyebrows. "It could be the detective."

"Not her ringtone." It was just the standard ringtone that came with the phone's unaltered settings and—

"That's your business line, though, right? Because it's your backup phone."

The phone stopped ringing. "Finish what you were saying."

"War—"

The phone rang again.

"Answer it." Worry darkened her eyes.

He yanked out the phone. Didn't recognize the number. "This had better be—" War began angrily because the caller had just interrupted probably the most important moment of his life.

"I know the cops are monitoring Rose's phone," a rasping voice told him. "I figured it would be wise for me to call you and deliver my message."

War's teeth ground together.

"I'm guessing Rose is close?"

Right in front of him. The little line between her eyebrows was deepening with her worry.

"You like to keep her close, don't you?" A taunt.

"Yes," he growled.

"That's made things difficult for me. You see, I wanted Rose close, too."

"Go screw yourself. You're not touching her."

Rose flinched.

"Thought you might say something along those lines," the disguised voice told him. "That's why, for tonight, I have turned my attention elsewhere. Another target came into my line of vision, thanks to you. Someone who deserves exactly what she will get."

"Who the hell are you talking about?" His heart pounded too fast.

"Don't worry, I'm sure her death will make for a killer headline on the news. She won't be behind the scenes any longer. She'll be the lead."

Click.

"War? What's happening?"

"Bastard said he has a new target. He's taunting me."

"That's what he did to me. He—he gave me clues. Wanted me to find his victim before he killed her." She grabbed him with her left hand. "*Tell me exactly what he said to you.*"

"Told me not to worry." *Such a confident dick.* "He said her death would make a killer headline. Then...something about her not being behind the scenes anymore. That she'd be leading." He swore. "Said she'd come into his line of vision because of me."

"Then it's someone who has been in contact with you lately. It's someone we've seen. If she works behind the scenes—*oh, no!*" Her voice rose. "It's Simone! We were talking to her today at the station. She fired Dylan. Simone works behind the scenes and—"

He was already calling Detective Slater as he spun for the door.

"She was going home," Rose rushed to say. "Simone told me—after we wrapped up the broadcast—that she was going home for the rest of the night."

Lynn answered his call on the second ring. He immediately said, "Get patrols over to Simone Davis's house. The perp just called—

"What? I wasn't told he'd contacted Rose! I've got people monitoring her phone. They should have contacted me immediately."

"He didn't use her phone. He called me." Tricky SOB. "Based on what he said, Rose thinks he is going after Simone."

"Why does she think that?"

He was bounding down the steps. Rose was bounding right behind him.

"Because he's dropping freaking clues, and she's the only one that fits." The only one that came to mind. He spared a glance over his shoulder. Rose had grabbed her phone, and she had it to her ear as she ran with him.

"I can't get her to answer!" Rose said, tone frantic. "Simone won't pick up!"

Shit. "We could be wrong," he told Lynn. "I want the guy to be lying to us. I don't want him going after anyone." But the perp was a piece of work. "We need uniforms at her home."

"On it."

He hung up and jumped in the car.

So did Rose.

Swearing, he turned toward her.

"Do not even start with me. You are not leaving me behind. Simone is my friend. We're helping her." She pointed straight ahead. "Drive. I'll give you directions. I know exactly where she lives and a shortcut to get there. *Let's go.*"

He floored it. They raced down the road.

"He wasn't supposed to go after anyone else. He was supposed to stay focused on *me*. If something happens to Simone..." Guilt thickened her words.

"It's not. It's okay. We're going to get to her."

She rattled off directions. "We're about ten minutes away."

Ten minutes was too damn far.

"I'm trying her phone again. I won't stop trying to get her. And the cops have to be closer than we are, right?"

It only took a few moments to die. The cops might not be close enough. And it might already be too late. The perp could have killed Simone *before* he called War. The whole scene could be a setup. But he didn't say any of those things to Rose. There was too much desperate hope in her voice. Hope that he couldn't shatter. "I'm sure they are close," he replied instead.

From the corner of his eye, he saw her shove her phone to her ear once more.

"Please, answer," Rose whispered. "Please, please..."

His car raced forward. His grip was too tight around the wheel. Simone had fired Dylan. But Dylan was still in custody. Just like he'd been in custody when Rose got her last call from the killer.

*It's not freaking Dylan.*

Who else would want to punish Simone? Who else would think she had to get what she deserved? These attacks—they were personal. War could see that.

"Please," Rose whispered again. "Come on, Simone, just pick up—*Simone!*" Relief had her voice breaking. "Simone, are you all right? Are you alone?" Her breath rushed out. "Listen, get to the most secure room in your house. The cops are on their way over. *Get there now.* Why? Because the freak after me—we think he might be after you, too." Her finger swiped over the phone and turned on the speaker.

*"OhmyGod."* Simone's terrified voice. "Why? Why me?"

"Get to a secure room," Rose urged her. "Go!"

"Is he in the house? Do you think he's already here?"

*I sure as hell hope not.*

"I'm in my bathroom. I'm locking the door. I-I didn't see anyone when I was running down the hall."

"The cops are coming. War and I are coming. It's going to be okay," Rose assured her. "You are going to be okay. I am going to talk to you the whole time. Nothing bad is going to happen. We're going to keep you safe..."

# CHAPTER NINETEEN

"I hear something." Simone's tremulous words filled the interior of War's car.

"We're almost there," Rose told her. "Two blocks. Just two more blocks. You're going to be fine." She couldn't consider any other option. They'd made it this far. Simone was going to be all right. "I can see your house."

Silence.

*"Simone!"* Blue lights flashed up ahead.

"I hear voices." A low whisper.

"It's the cops. I see their lights. War is braking the car. I'm coming in. Simone, it's going to be okay. Everything is okay!" She didn't hang up. Even as she and War jumped from the car and ran with the cops to Simone's house, Rose didn't stop talking.

"I'm coming to meet you," Simone said. "I'm unlocking the bathroom door. I'm coming out. You're there? Promise, you're there?"

"I'm here." Almost at her station manager's front door. "I promise."

Seconds later, that front door was ripped open. Simone—wearing gray sweats and a matching top—stood trembling on the threshold.

"Ma'am, we want to search the house," one of the cops said.

Simone gave a jerky nod. "Do it. Do—" She threw herself against Rose. Held on tight. "I have never been so scared in my whole life!"

Rose gripped her just as fiercely. Simone was safe. *Alive.* Rose hadn't gotten there too late this time. They'd made a difference.

"You need to get someone to sweep the neighborhood." War's low voice reached her ears, and she knew he was talking to the cops. "Make sure the bastard isn't lurking around, watching the scene. He could have been coming but stopped when he saw the blue lights."

Simone shuddered.

"You shouldn't stay here tonight," Rose told her as Simone continued to grip her tightly. "We need to get you somewhere safe."

Simone pulled back, but she didn't let go of Rose. "I will be staying in freaking Fort Knox, I can assure you of that." The light from her porch fell on her face and showed her strained expression. "Is this what it's been like for you? The fear eating through you? Being so scared your whole body shakes?"

Rose nodded. Yes, that was exactly what it had been like. "He won't get you."

"I don't want him getting *either* of us."

Yes, that was a wonderful plan.

\*\*\*

"No sign of the perp." The detective's frustration was clear. "Neighbors didn't see anything. All the security cameras in this fancy neighborhood didn't pick up jack. Either our guy is very, very good at evasion—"

"Or he was never here," Rose finished.

Lynn nodded. "Your friend said she had a secure location she could use for the night. I'm going to keep uniforms on her, and I want to extend that same offer to you." She motioned toward a silent War. "I get that he's shadowing you, but if you want to come into protective custody—"

"Why did he want us racing over here?" Rose wondered. "Don't get me wrong. I am thrilled that Simone is okay." Thrilled. Relieved. Grateful to the depths of her very soul. "And, sure, he is good at evasion. He's gotten away with his crimes for a long time. He obviously knows security. Knows how to stay in the shadows. Knows how to make sure he isn't seen when he doesn't want to be."

War stiffened.

"But...if he wasn't going after Simone, if he didn't get scared off...if giving War that call was all a red herring...why?" The question wouldn't stop nagging at her.

"Maybe he wanted you out in the open." Lynn's gaze drifted down the street. A few watchful neighbors still stood on their carefully edged and mowed lawns as they watched the scene. "And with that in mind, I think it's time you left." Her attention slid to War. "When you go back home, you'll make sure you have no tails?

He nodded.

"Watch your ass," Lynn directed curtly.

"I always do." His head angled to the left. "Dylan is still in custody, that's what you told me?"

"I'm letting him cool his heels for a while, yes."

"Can you ask him a question for me?"

She winced. "He lawyered up again. But we'll see what I can do." A pause. "What's the question?"

"Ask him if—when he was in Tampa at that conference—he spent the night drinking with a PI named Gary Strom."

Lynn groaned. "Not Sex Pic Strom. Tell me that jerk isn't involved in this mess."

"According to Gary, he's Dylan's alibi for the Tampa murder."

Lynn's hands went to her hips. The movement had her holster shifting a little on her side. "Dylan didn't mention an alibi for that crime. Hell, he wouldn't tell me anything about his whereabouts. His lawyer shut things down, fast."

"I would think his lawyer would want you to know if Dylan had an alibi that would clear him." Keeping an alibi secret didn't make sense to Rose.

"You would think that, wouldn't you?" Lynn returned. "Unless the alibi is bullshit." One of the uniforms called her name. "Got to go. You hear anything else from this freak, you call me, got it?"

"You are at the top of our phone contact list," Rose assured her.

Lynn hurried toward the waiting cops.

The wind caught Rose's hair and tossed locks against her cheek. Shivering, she pushed them back. When she turned her head, she found War staring at her. He was in shadows so it was hard for her to see his expression but... "What is it?"

He took her hand. Led her to the car. He made sure she was settled first, and she noticed him sweeping quick stares around the scene before he climbed in behind the driver's seat.

"War." She touched his arm. "I can practically feel your thoughts spinning. What is going on?"

"The alibi...it protected Dylan *and* Gary."

It was like he'd read her mind. "I was thinking the same thing. I was also thinking that—if the alibi was real, Dylan definitely would have mentioned it. But he didn't. Gary did, and that sure seemed convenient." Something else that was convenient... "He was ready to throw Billy under the bus. And the PI obviously has no trouble with lies, so it's not like I believe he and the truth are closely affiliated."

His head turned toward her. "You in the mood for a pitstop on the way home?"

She grabbed the seatbelt. "If that pitstop means we are going to do some B&E at Gary's office, then absolutely I am."

"We have to talk about your criminal tendencies..."

Nerves had her practically twitching. "Let's talk about them after we search his place and see if Sex Pic Strom has other secrets he's been keeping." Like the kind of secrets a person would kill to hide.

\*\*\*

"Are you going to pick the lock?" Rose asked eagerly as she crowded in behind War.

He hated to disappoint her but... "Nah. I'm going to use the key."

"What?"

He flashed her a quick grin, despite the grim situation. "I might have snuck the key while we were fighting earlier. I snagged the key to this place and the key to the big-ass filing cabinet he has inside."

"The cabinet that collided with your knuckles?"

"Same one," he assured her. "I also scoped out the office for security cameras and discovered that unless he likes very, very small surveillance tech, then we're clear." Having small tech was a possibility. Cameras could be practically invisible these days. But his instincts told him Gary didn't want footage of his own office. Probably because he worked too many shady deals that might bite him in the ass. And if Gary's clients were to ever discover that they'd been filmed...

*That wouldn't go so well for you, would it, Gary?*

They slipped inside. War went straight for the filing cabinet. Rose headed for the desk. She turned on the lamp. Eased open some desk drawers. They were both wearing gloves. Starting to make a habit of their B&Es. "Maybe we should try a date," he said as the filing cabinet's top drawer screeched open. "Instead of just joint criminal activity."

She turned toward him. She held what looked like a small datebook in her hands. "He had an appointment with Michael Post several months ago."

He flipped through the files in the drawer.

"Michael is Janet Post's *ex*-husband," Rose said. "I met him twice. Once was the day after I found Janet's body. He seemed torn up. Gutted by her death."

He found a file labeled *Post*. War pulled it out. Thumbed through the continents. "Torn up? Interesting. Because the guy hired Gary to find proof that his wife had been cheating on him during their marriage. He was convinced she'd fooled the judge. That she'd fooled him."

Rose put down the datebook and hurried closer. "Gary was watching Janet?"

Yes, and that was a huge red flag.

"What about Barbara Briggs?" Rose asked. She reached into the filing cabinet.

*Briggs.*

There was a file there for her, too.

Rose pulled it out. Studied the photos. "He was tailing her." She thumbed through them. Found a note. "Her fiancé hired him. He thought Barbara was hiding something from him." Rose shook her head. "But she's not with anyone else in these pictures. She's just going to work. Shopping. She's not cheating or doing anything wrong at all."

No, she wasn't. Those pictures... "They're like the ones that Dylan had in his drawer of you."

She put down the file. "Give me the file that Gary has on me."

Ah, about that... "So, Rose—"

She snagged the file labeled *Shadow*. Rose yanked it open. *"Oh. My. God."*

He winced.

"That's me."

"Not exactly."

She yanked one of the photos up high and peered at it. "That is an excellent photoshopping job."

"Barely mediocre."

Her fingers balled up the photo. Only there were plenty more waiting. "You've seen these."

A roll of one shoulder. He'd mentioned the photos back at his place. Told her they were BS.

"That's what led to the whole incident with your fist hitting the filing cabinet? You saw *these* photos?" She eyed the dent in the side of the filing cabinet.

"I knew they were fake."

"They are exceedingly good fakes. Who knew Gary had those skills?"

"Personally, I thought the man had zero skills. I'm also still not impressed."

Rose exhaled on a rough sigh. "How did you know they weren't real?"

"Because you told me that you hadn't been with anyone since me." She'd told him. He believed her. "Gary wanted me to think those had been taken since we broke up." A shrug. "He was lying."

"Yes. He was."

"I told you before, baby, it's you. I believe you. I choose you. I will always stand with you." Another roll of his shoulder. "He started being a dick after that point." *Started?* Ha. The man was always a dick. "If you want the truth, I called him on his bullshit, and in response, he pulled a gun on me."

She flinched.

"It wasn't loaded." He'd told her this before. "Said he just used it to protect himself. That he didn't like guns."

She shoved the *Shadow* file back into the drawer.

"Was easy enough to get the gun away. His mistake was pulling it when I was so close to him."

She bit her lower lip. "If he faked those pictures of me..." Her gaze darted to the filing cabinet. "Then maybe he's faked a ton more. Maybe he's ruined lives and never looked back." She started thumbing through the files. "*War.*"

He jerked to attention at the alarm in her voice.

She looked at him. "Every single victim is here. He has a file on every victim that I know about."

War moved closer to get a better look. A few moments later, he realized—yes, Rose was right. Gary had been hired to do surveillance work on the women who'd later been strangled. He'd been watching them, and they'd been found dead. "That is no coincidence."

Rose backed up a step. "It's a massive filing cabinet. I bet every drawer is full of cases." Her voice thickened. "What if there are more victims?" Fear and horror had her paling. "War, what if there were *more*?"

Swearing, War pulled out his phone. The cops needed to be brought in, now. The phone rang, then, "Lynn? You need to bring in Gary Strom for questioning."

"Ugh. Him. Why?"

Staring straight at Rose, War said, "Because an anonymous source just told you that Gary was hired to tail all of the murder victims on the case you're working…"

***

"The cops are going to find him." War killed the headlights and propped his arm on the steering wheel as he angled toward Rose. "This is the intel we needed, baby. They are going to get Gary, and the nightmare will be over."

*Freaking Gary Strom.* Now that War looked back, it made sense. Gary had watched his victims, stalked them, and then killed them.

He'd kept the case files and all the photos like some kind of sick trophies.

The significant others who had hired Gary hadn't told the police about him because they hadn't wanted to air the dirty laundry about their dead. Or maybe they'd felt guilty for being suspicious in the first place. Whatever their reasons had been, their silence had allowed Gary to slip past detection.

He wasn't slipping away any longer.

The cops were on their way to Gary's house. War had wanted to be there, too, but Lynn had ordered him to stand down. She'd pulled the official police business card on him. That shit hadn't been cool.

Nothing about this case had been cool.

"I could use a drink," Rose told him. "What about you?"

Oh, he could use a few things. A drink. Her. Her answering the question that had been left hanging between them the last time they'd been at his house...

*You have my ring, sweetheart. What can I do to have you?*

He would be patient. He could do this. Use his self-control for something good. He'd *woo* her. He was pretty sure that was a thing. Take her out. Show her the time of her life. Make her forget every other jackass she'd ever known. *Wooing.*

"War? What is it?"

He shook his head. "Let's get that drink." He climbed from the car. The waves slammed into the shore, and the scent of the salt water teased his nose. Rose came to meet him, and his fingers curled with hers.

He loved this beach. Loved this place. After he'd entered civilian life, it had been a needed balm for his psyche. Nightmares had plagued him at first. Memories of people he couldn't save. People he'd killed.

Some nights, he would even sleep on the beach. He'd stare up at the stars and dream of what life could be like.

His gaze drifted to Rose as he headed for the cabin.

*I love this beach. I love this home. I love this woman.*

"I'd like to finish our conversation from earlier," Rose told him. "About the ring?"

The waves thundered. The water was rough that night. Loud. He could barely hear her over the crash of the waves.

"Because there is something you should know." Rose turned toward him as they stood at the foot of the stairs that led up to his cabin.

He squared his shoulders. Waited.

"I want a life with you, War. I want to stay with you. Grow old with you. Have every crazy kind of adventure with you. I love you, and I want us to have a second chance."

Fuck...*yes*. He wanted all of that. Every single thing. Mostly, he just wanted...*her*.

"This mess is almost over." Her body moved closer to his. Pressed to his. "How about we start planning for our future? Let's focus on the good things that will come."

"You are the best thing in my life." The thing that mattered most. His head lowered. His lips feathered over hers. As always, she tasted so sweet. So delicious. He wanted to eat her alive.

*Rose said she loves me.* She was giving them a second chance. Not slamming the door shut on the dreams he'd had. They could do this. It could all work out. Not turn to ashes in his hands.

"Let's get inside." Where it was safe. Where they could be alone because Odin was sleeping at the apartment above Armageddon. They could go inside where he could strip her and kiss every single inch of her body. Where he could have her...

*Always.*

*Forever.*

She eased back from him. "Everything is going to be okay now."

Damn straight.

He threaded his fingers with hers. They climbed up the steps. His chest felt lighter. The heavy, pressing weight on his heart was finally gone. The cops would pick up Gary. Rose would be safe. He and Rose could start their new life.

*Trust. Love.* They had it all.

They hurried onto the screened-in porch. The light was shining there. Rose was smiling. A grin that bloomed on her face and lit her eyes. She was absolutely beautiful. She took his breath away. Commanded his heart.

She *owned* his heart, and there was nothing that he wouldn't do for her. They rushed across the porch and were soon at the door that led inside. He unlocked it, and they stepped over the threshold. Rose was sliding her hand up his chest and smiling at him. So happy and beautiful, but—

Something was off.

*The alarm?* It hadn't beeped.

"The gun's loaded this time," a rough, male voice announced.

He looked up and saw Gary sitting on the couch, with a gun aimed at War and Rose.

War shoved her behind him even as he heard the thunder of that weapon. Rose screamed. Fire burned in War's chest, and he could feel the wetness of his blood.

Gary fired again.

"No!" Rose yelled.

War was sagging, his body falling. He...*fuck.* "Run," he told Rose.

She shook her head. She grabbed for him.

The gun blasted again.

# CHAPTER TWENTY

Gary laughed even as more blood coated War's chest. "Don't worry, Rose. I don't plan to use the gun on you. I *hate* guns. So impersonal. There is no pleasure in killing someone from a distance. Just doesn't give you the same release."

Rose had her hands pressed to War's chest. Tears streamed down her face as she frantically tried to staunch the flow of blood.

Why the hell wasn't she leaving? War's breath sawed in and out. "*Go.*"

Rose shook her head. "I am staying with you—"

"I'll just end this," Gary told her as he stalked closer. "Put him out of his misery. Then you won't have to worry about whether you leave him behind or not."

Rose was on her knees beside War. His chest was burning. Warm blood had soaked his shirt.

Over her shoulder, War saw Gary and the bastard's sick smirk. He was raising his gun, and War knew the prick was going to shoot him again. *So much for hating guns, huh, Gary? Or do you just like to use them when you know your prey is strong enough to kick your ass and you have to shoot him to take him down?*

War's fingers flexed. He had his knife in his boot. If he could just get it—

Gary inched closer.

*No time.* War wouldn't be able to get the knife out. "Rose..." he growled.

Her hands flew back and she grabbed Gary's legs. She shoved her whole body against him, and he slammed into the floor. The gun flew from his fingers and slid under the couch.

"G-get...away," War forced the words out. The room was getting dark. Weakness slid through him. Rose had to get out of there. She had to escape.

But she was diving toward the couch. Stretching her hands under it as she tried to find the gun—

And War saw Gary grab her.

***

She could see the butt of the gun. Rose stretched her hand to reach it. Just a little bit more—

A hard hand clamped around her ankle and wrenched her back. Screaming, Rose flipped over. Gary—with a triumphant expression on his face and his puffy lips twisted in an evil grin—had a death grip on her right ankle. Her left was still free, so she slammed her left foot into his face. As hard as she could. Twice. Three times. She kept kicking him in the face until he let her go. Then Rose sprang to her feet and ran for the kitchen. "You want me?" she screamed at him. "Come get me!"

Because she didn't want him in there with War. She didn't want the bastard anywhere near War.

*War is fine. It looked worse than it was. He is fine.* Multiple gunshot wounds—he was totally fine. He *had* to be fine. There was no other option.

War was fine, and maybe she was hysterical and in shock, but who the hell cared?

She grabbed a butcher knife from the knife block and whirled. Gary was steps behind her. "Don't even think about it," she warned him.

He smiled. Held up his hands. "Think about what? Killing you? I assure you, it's all I've been thinking about since I was first hired to watch you."

"You were hired to watch all of your victims!"

He didn't deny the charge. Instead, he said, "Maybe if they'd been faithful, they wouldn't have needed to be punished."

"Don't give me your bullshit! This isn't about them—those women did nothing wrong." Her hold on the knife tightened. "You're the freak who stalked them and killed them. I saw the photoshopped pictures you had of me. How many times did you lie to your clients? How many times did you invent cheating that never happened?"

His grin stretched. "Those were good pics of you, weren't they? Thought for sure they'd send your jackass of a lover over the edge."

Her gaze darted to War. Because the kitchen opened straight to the den, she could see him.

When she looked back at Gary, he'd taken a step closer to her. "Don't you do it," she ordered. "I will stab you."

"But what will one stab do? Because it's unlikely that you'll kill me with one blow."

*Don't count on it.*

"Then I'll have you. I'll take that knife from you. I don't like knives. Not a big fan of blood. Messes up the moment, if you will. Though, your boyfriend is currently covered in blood, isn't he?"

He was trying to get her to look at War again. Her gaze stayed on Gary. "If you didn't like blood, then maybe you shouldn't have shot him."

His smile slipped. "He wasn't supposed to be here. He left you behind last time. Came to my office alone. He was so worried about you being at risk that I was sure he would make you stay here. I know his blond friend was sleeping above the bar."

How did he know? Had he put a camera near Armageddon? Been watching the place?

"It should have been so easy. When I was here before, I scoped the place out. Once I figured out the best way to get inside, it was just going to be about sneaking in and getting my rope around your neck." He lowered his right hand. Reached into the oversized pocket of his coat. Pulled out a black, nylon rope. It was then she realized he was wearing gloves. "War would have come back and found you dead. Quite tragic, but at least he would have still been alive. Now he's dead, and that's on you."

*Now he's dead.*

Her stare flew to War. He wasn't moving. A sob choked from her. There was so much blood on him, and War's big body was chillingly still. No, no—

Gary grabbed her.

"*No!*" Rose screamed. She sliced down with her knife, and it drove into his shoulder. Blood spurted and flew at her, and she wrenched back the knife to stab him again.

He shoved her back, and her shoulders slammed into the refrigerator.

"Your boyfriend taught me this trick." He had her wrist, and he was pounding it into the wall. Over and over. The knife fell as her fingers went numb and pain exploded in her wrist. She tried to knee him, but he'd angled his legs between hers. "Don't worry." His breath blew over her face. "I think it will feel good for you. At the end, when your brain is deprived of oxygen, you'll feel a surge of bliss. I'll give you that. I'll give you the most perfect moment of your life."

No, he wouldn't. Because he was insane. She went for his eyes with her free hand.

He jerked his head back, and her fingers fumbled over his cheek. She didn't have any good nails—she kept them too short, an old habit. If she had nails, she would have been digging them into him.

He let go. The move was so sudden that she staggered. Her breath huffed out, and she jerked toward—

He had the rope around her neck. He'd moved so fast. A lightning-quick movement.

"Not the first time I've done this," he said as he leaned in close. His breath blew over her cheek. "You learn how to get your vic where you want her. How to distract, then move in for the kill."

Her fingers grabbed at the rope, but it was too tight. She couldn't pull it away, and it was cutting into her throat. Digging into her skin. Rose could hear a frantic pounding in her head.

It was like before...when she'd been in the bathroom of that cheap motel. She'd heard that terrible pounding as she fought for her life. She'd been terrified. Her vision had begun to go blurry...

He was keeping his eyes away from her. She couldn't gouge out that bastard's eyes. She—she—

*He's stronger than you. So you have to be smarter.*

Her frantic struggles were just egging him on. His breath was fast, and his feverish gaze burned with excitement. He liked her fight.

She stopped fighting.

"What—what are you doing?"

She stared straight into his gaze. He'd stopped squeezing when she stopped struggling.

"Do you *want* to die?" Spittle flew from his mouth.

No, she didn't want to die. She wanted to live a long and happy life with War. Maybe have a kid or two. Definitely get a pug. She wanted to walk along the beach at sunset. She wanted to make love with War under the moonlight. Rose had a million things on her to-do list. And dying?

Not on that list.

She let her hands fall limply to her sides.

*"What the fuck are you doing?"* Gary leaned in closer once more. Brought his snarling face right before hers.

Her fingers slid into her pocket. Curled around the ring that she'd put there earlier. The ring War had given to her. Her ring.

"You're not making this any good!"

Oh, she was screwing this up for him? Great.

His lips pulled back as he bared his teeth at her and began to tighten the rope once more—

Her left hand flew up. She gripped the ring tightly and she raked the diamond across his face as hard as she could.

He screamed and backed up. A stumbling step. She flew to the side and raced away from the kitchen. The rope was still around her throat, but she wasn't going to slow down, she was going to—

*War.*

She almost ran straight into him. He was on his feet. Right near the kitchen. Weaving a little, but upright. Still covered in blood. But *up.* "War?"

He grabbed her. Shoved her behind him. "G-go. Told you...*g-go*..." He yanked the rope off her neck. "Call...cops..."

"I will kill you both!" Gary promised. "You first, then her!"

"No." That's all War said. Just a deep, hard rumble.

A guttural yell broke from Gary. He surged toward War with his fists swinging.

War didn't move at all. Rose was diving toward the couch and the gun that was still under it. She could get the gun and stop Gary. She could help War. She could—

Gary thudded into the floor near her.

She screamed and twisted her body.

War was straddled over him, and War pounded his fist into Gary's face over and over. Gary was trying to fight back, but it was like watching someone swat ineffectively at a fly. His blows just seemed to rain off War.

Then War took the black rope, and he wrapped it around Gary's neck. He tightened it as fear flooded into Gary's expression.

"How does...that feel?" War grated.

Gary's mouth hung open. Croaking noises emerged from him as his face became blood-red.

War didn't let him go. Gary was still swinging at War, but his swats became even weaker. So weak that soon his hands fell to the floor.

His mouth was still wide open. So were his eyes.

She pushed up to her knees. "War?"

He didn't look her way. "Call...cops."

"War, he's dying."

He didn't let go.

"War..." She inched toward him.

Gary's body had just gone limp. He'd lost consciousness. How long would it take for him to die? "He's not fighting."

"He...shouldn't be living. He..." War swallowed. "I won't...last longer...have to make sure...no threat...you."

He wouldn't last longer? Oh, the hell, he wouldn't. He was going to last for the next fifty years. At least. Sixty. Seventy would be fabulous. "War, let him go."

He didn't.

She jumped to her feet. Searched quickly and frantically and found the handcuffs that Odin had brought back to them. Rose raced to War, and she grabbed his arms. "Let go." Because she could see—more clearly than ever—that his control was gone. War was operating on pure animal instinct.

His main instinct? It was to protect her. To eliminate any threat to her.

That threat wasn't moving.

"War...*look at me.*"

War's gaze lifted to her face. His dark stare seemed unfocused. Lost.

"He's out. He won't hurt me." She wrenched up Gary's hands and cuffed them. "He's secure. Let him go so I can take care of *you.*"

"You...safe?"

"I am."

His white-knuckled grip eased. As the rope loosened, her fingers slid to Gary's throat. There was a weak, thready pulse. The bastard was still alive.

War fell back.

She grabbed for him. "War!"

His breath heaved out. "That's...lot of blood."

It was an insane amount of blood. Enough to have her losing her mind. She needed to put pressure on his wounds, but she also had to call for help because War needed an ambulance and Gary needed a cop car. She managed to find a phone, and Rose dialed nine-one-one with shaky fingers. It was only when she was giving the address to the emergency dispatcher that Rose realized her voice sounded like a raspy croak and that her throat burned and throbbed.

She put that pain out of her mind. It didn't matter. Nothing but War mattered. The cops were coming. An ambulance was coming. War would be okay. No other option existed for her.

Her hands pushed against his chest. His blood immediately seeped through her fingers.

"Rose?"

"What is it?" When he didn't respond and his eyes sagged shut, she yelled, "War!"

"Love...you."

"I love you, too, so don't you *dare* think of dying on me. Do you hear me? War? War? So help me...if you die on me, I will make you sorry that you were ever born." Tears poured but she ignored them and kept up the pressure on his chest. "You don't want to piss me off. So don't you die. Please, War, *please*. Don't die!"

# CHAPTER TWENTY-ONE

"You're a lucky sonofabitch, you know that?" Odin helped himself to the yogurt on War's hospital food tray. "You nab the killer, you get the girl, and you score more scars so your rep looks extra tough. Wins all around for you."

War pulled his gaze away from the TV screen. His favorite reporter was about to come on the air. He didn't want to miss the next segment but... "I wanted to kill him."

Odin shoveled the chocolate yogurt in his mouth. "Why didn't you?"

"Rose."

Because she'd been staring at him. Eyes terrified. Body trembling. A red line around her neck from where the rope had been.

It had taken all of War's strength to get off that floor and go after Gary. But there was no way he would have let Rose die. "I think she didn't want me having his death on my conscience or something like that."

Odin made a face.

"I know. My conscience would have been just fine." He risked a glance at the TV. She wasn't on yet. "But there were vics the cops didn't know about. A whole hell of a lot more. That sick freak was at this for a while."

"I hear there won't be any deals for him." Odin put down the empty cup.

"Not a damn one." He'd get life in prison or death row. A jury would decide his fate. "I wanted that yogurt."

"Um."

War shook his head. He saw the segment he'd been waiting on pop up. War grabbed the remote and turned up the volume.

"Gary Strom has admitted to stalking and murdering eleven women," Rose said as she stood in front of the courthouse. Her voice was grim, sad. "His confession came following a police search of his office—a search that uncovered records of his attacks dating back five years."

"Five years," Odin repeated. "Jesus."

War didn't look away from the screen.

"Gary Strom would stalk his prey relentlessly. Document his hunts with photos. Then close in for the kill." Her solemn gaze stared into the camera. "I was one of his victims. A victim lucky enough to survive thanks to the incredible bravery of a man named Warren Channing."

"Aw, she called you Warren."

"Shut the hell up." She was wearing the ring. The ring that *had* been in evidence for a while, but they had just managed to get back. Lynn had pulled strings for them. He'd seriously owe her.

"Warren Channing is a private investigator with Trouble For Hire, and his help was instrumental in apprehending Strom."

"Oh, look," Odin sounded impressed. "She makes it sound nice. Like you didn't nearly choke the life from that SOB in a blind rage."

"Wasn't blind. I could see perfectly." He'd known exactly what he was doing. *Killing to protect. Killing to destroy the threat. Killing...because Rose had to be safe.*

"I'm speaking out tonight because I want the world to know what happened to me. What happened to all of those women." Rose lifted her chin. "It is estimated that one in six women will experience stalking at some point. If you are a victim, you don't need to suffer and fear in silence. You can get help. You can fight. You can stop the monsters out there."

"I like her."

War's gaze cut to Odin.

His friend was staring straight at the screen.

"I like her, too," War said.

"Notice she's wearing your ring."

He inclined his head. "Good of you to see that."

"When's the wedding?"

"As soon as I can get her in a church."

"Do I get to be the best man?"

"You know it."

Odin smiled.

And War went back to watching his favorite reporter. God, he loved that woman.

***

"You are getting way too much joy out of this whole deal," War grumbled as his hands clamped around the arms of his wheelchair.

"Aw, someone is grumpy," Rose announced in a perky voice.

He turned his head so he could glare back at her. "I am more than capable of walking."

"Yes, but the lovely folks at the hospital have a policy against that, so you have to be pushed out until your sweet feet hit the curb. I volunteered to push so...enjoy the ride." She smiled at him.

He got caught by her smile. Couldn't look away. Didn't want to stare anywhere else. Rose was happy. She was safe.

Everything was right in his world.

"What were the doctor's orders?" she asked as she pushed him through the sliding glass doors that had just opened. "Are you, um, supposed to avoid any certain activities?"

Oh, that was precious. She thought he'd be avoiding his favorite activity? No way in hell. "Supposed to take things slow," he replied as his head turned forward once more. "I figure you can be on top, and I can watch as you slowly ride—"

"War!"

Now it was his turn to smile. "You don't like that plan?" His car was waiting at the curb. She'd driven it. Did she know that she was the only other person he'd ever allowed to drive his baby?

"I love that plan," Rose whispered as her mouth slid against his ear. "Can't wait to get you home so we can start enjoying that plan."

He figured he was close enough to the curb. War shoved out of the chair.

"No, War!" She reached for him. "What if you fall?" She locked her arms around him.

He had fallen—fast and hard for her. He turned. His head bent toward her and his mouth brushed over her lips. She was with him. Safe. Alive. He had everything that he would ever need.

"Let's go home," Rose murmured.

He was home. A kid who'd lost his family. A fighter who'd slipped in and out of more countries than he could count. But he'd finally found his home—and it wasn't the cabin or the beach or anything but...*her*. Rose was his home.

She was his heart.

***

Their clothes littered the floor. Not like they'd wasted time stripping. War was reaching for her again, but Rose caught his hands and pushed them back down. "I think you don't understand the meaning of slow and easy."

He grinned at her, and her chest warmed. His smile was sexy and charming, and she loved him so much that she felt like her whole body might explode with joy.

She'd been so worried about him. They'd gone back to his cabin—Odin had made sure there were no signs of the attack. Odin had been such a good friend. He'd given her some much support while she'd stayed at War's side during those days at the hospital. The doctors had told her not to worry, that he'd been lucky, that War was a fighter...

But she hadn't been able to shake her fear. Not until they finally drove away from the hospital and it was in her rear-view mirror.

The pain and the fear and that jerk Gary—they were all in her rear-view. What was on the road in front of her, her future—that was War.

"You are torturing me," he groaned.

"No, I am being extra..." Her fingers released their grip on his hands as she moved to trace a light path down his chest. "Gentle." She made sure not to touch any of his healing injuries. Down, down her careful fingers went...

Until she was stroking the long, hard length of his cock. Her hand curled around him, and she squeezed. Squeezed and released before she began to pump—

*"Rose."* His eyes had darkened even more.

"So gentle," she said. Her body shifted so that she could bring her mouth down and feather a kiss over the head of his cock.

He growled and his hips jerked up.

She slowly opened her mouth. Took a little of him inside. One inch. Two.

*"Torture..."*

She took more. Swirled her tongue over him. Sucked.

*"Rose!"* He'd fisted the sheets. "There is slow," he gritted out, "then there is making-me-lose-my-mind torture!"

She didn't want him losing his mind. Couldn't very well have that. She rose and straddled him. The tip of his cock pressed to her core. She stared into his eyes and sank down.

Slowly.

That had been the plan, correct?

One careful inch at a time.

His jaw locked. "Fuck me!"

"I am."

A choked laugh barked from him. His hands let go of their tight grip on the sheets and flew to curl around her hips. "More, Rose. *More.*"

Her knees pressed against the mattress. She pushed up. Sank back down.

A guttural groan came from him. His hands lifted her up. Urged her down. Faster...

War was forgetting that they were supposed to be going slow. He was attempting to take over and change the plan. "War..."

His right hand slid away from her hip. Moved lower down her body. His fingers rubbed over her clit.

Her breath jerked out.

She pushed up. Sank down. His fingers kept strumming her. She was staring straight at him. His burning gaze was on her. The thunder of her heart grew louder and louder, and her climax built within her. She could feel it driving through her. Every thrust had her closer and closer to the edge. So close that—

She went over. Pleasure poured through her, and she shoved down against him, taking him in as deeply as she could. War was climaxing with her. She could feel it—feel him. He poured into her even as his hips jerked and heaved against her.

Her hands flew back to push against his thighs so she could hold her balance. War had *strong* thighs. Strong everything. She let the orgasm consume them both.

She enjoyed the hell out of that ride.

When her heart slowed, when her breathing evened, she opened her eyes to find him staring at her.

And smiling.

His expression—there was just so much love on his face. She'd never quite had anyone look at her the way War did.

"You're wearing the ring." His voice was husky, thick, and satisfied.

Her left hand lifted. She didn't get off him. She enjoyed her seat far too much. "This ring?" She wiggled her fingers. *Maybe* tightened her inner muscles around him.

"*Rose*. God. Yes. That ring."

"I am wearing it." Another slow clench.

"When are you...*that feels so good...*"

He was already getting hard inside of her again. He must definitely be feeling better.

"When are you...gonna marry me?" His head had tilted to the left against the pillow as he stared up at her.

She tapped her chin. "Well, that depends..."

"On?"

"On how fast you can get me a church reserved."

His head shifted to the right. He flashed her his killer grin. "Consider it done."

She leaned over him. Pressed a kiss to his lips. "I thought you might say something like that."

"What else do you need? Tell me. I can make it happen. I want a life with you. I want—"

"You," she told him before pressing another kiss to his lips. "You're the only thing I need." She wouldn't think of her fears any longer. Wouldn't think of terrible what-if scenarios for things that might have been. She was safe. War was safe. They had a future waiting—their future together. "You're what I need. You and me. Saying our vows and starting our life." That was everything for her.

"You've got me," he told her. "You'll always have me."

She liked the sound of his promise.

"I will love you, I will protect you, I will stand with you against anyone and everyone." He stared into her eyes. "You're it for me, baby. My end game. My once-in-a-lifetime."

That was sweet. Very un-War-like. "Maybe those should be your vows." He was still *in* her. Talking was getting hard. She wanted to do more moving. But—

"If they were," War rumbled, "what would yours be?"

She didn't look away from him. "I will love you, I will protect *you,* and I will stand with you against anyone and everyone."

He smiled.

"You're it for me, baby," she told him and shared a smile of her own. But her smile slowly faded. This mattered. He mattered. "You are my happily-ever-after. You are my safe place when the world is crazy. You are the one I turn to when I think I'm lost."

"I was lost without you." Gruff.

They weren't lost anymore. They'd found their way back to each other. They were stronger now. Better.

And they'd never get lost again.

**THE END**

# A NOTE FROM THE AUTHOR

Thank you for reading NO ESCAPE FROM WAR! I hope you enjoyed the story. I wanted to write a book that would be a fun mix of romance, humor, and suspense, and War's story just emerged! And there are more "Trouble for Hire" stories planned...War's friend Odin will have a book, too (DON'T PLAY WITH ODIN).

It was such fun to set NO ESCAPE FROM WAR in an area of the country that is near and dear to me. If you have never visited the beautiful Pensacola and Pensacola Beach area, you should add it to your list!

If you'd like to stay updated on my releases and sales, please join my newsletter list.

*https://cynthiaeden.com/newsletter/*

Again, thank you for reading NO ESCAPE FROM WAR.

Best,
Cynthia Eden
*cynthiaeden.com*

# ABOUT THE AUTHOR

Cynthia Eden is a *New York Times, USA Today, Digital Book World*, and *IndieReader* best-seller.

Cynthia writes sexy tales of contemporary romance, romantic suspense, and paranormal romance. Since she began writing full-time in 2005, Cynthia has written over one hundred novels and novellas.

Cynthia lives along the Alabama Gulf Coast. She loves romance novels, horror movies, and chocolate.

## For More Information
- *cynthiaeden.com*
- *facebook.com/cynthiaedenfanpage*

# HER OTHER WORKS

## Death and Moonlight Mystery
- Step Into My Web (Book 1)
- Save Me From The Dark (Book 2)

## Wilde Ways
- Protecting Piper (Book 1)
- Guarding Gwen (Book 2)
- Before Ben (Book 3)
- The Heart You Break (Book 4)
- Fighting For Her (Book 5)
- Ghost Of A Chance (Book 6)
- Crossing The Line (Book 7)
- Counting On Cole (Book 8)
- Chase After Me (Book 9)
- Say I Do (Book 10)
- Roman Will Fall (Book 11)
- The One Who Got Away (Book 12)

## Dark Sins
- Don't Trust A Killer (Book 1)
- Don't Love A Liar (Book 2)

## Lazarus Rising
- Never Let Go (Book One)
- Keep Me Close (Book Two)

- Stay With Me (Book Three)
- Run To Me (Book Four)
- Lie Close To Me (Book Five)
- Hold On Tight (Book Six)
- Lazarus Rising Volume One (Books 1 to 3)
- Lazarus Rising Volume Two (Books 4 to 6)

## Dark Obsession Series

- Watch Me (Book 1)
- Want Me (Book 2)
- Need Me (Book 3)
- Beware Of Me (Book 4)
- Only For Me (Books 1 to 4)

## Mine Series

- Mine To Take (Book 1)
- Mine To Keep (Book 2)
- Mine To Hold (Book 3)
- Mine To Crave (Book 4)
- Mine To Have (Book 5)
- Mine To Protect (Book 6)
- Mine Box Set Volume 1 (Books 1-3)
- Mine Box Set Volume 2 (Books 4-6)

## Bad Things

- The Devil In Disguise (Book 1)
- On The Prowl (Book 2)
- Undead Or Alive (Book 3)
- Broken Angel (Book 4)
- Heart Of Stone (Book 5)
- Tempted By Fate (Book 6)
- Wicked And Wild (Book 7)

- Saint Or Sinner (Book 8)
- Bad Things Volume One (Books 1 to 3)
- Bad Things Volume Two (Books 4 to 6)
- Bad Things Deluxe Box Set (Books 1 to 6)

## Bite Series

- Forbidden Bite (Bite Book 1)
- Mating Bite (Bite Book 2)

## Blood and Moonlight Series

- Bite The Dust (Book 1)
- Better Off Undead (Book 2)
- Bitter Blood (Book 3)
- Blood and Moonlight (The Complete Series)

## Purgatory Series

- The Wolf Within (Book 1)
- Marked By The Vampire (Book 2)
- Charming The Beast (Book 3)
- Deal with the Devil (Book 4)
- The Beasts Inside (Books 1 to 4)

## Bound Series

- Bound By Blood (Book 1)
- Bound In Darkness (Book 2)
- Bound In Sin (Book 3)
- Bound By The Night (Book 4)
- Bound in Death (Book 5)
- Forever Bound (Books 1 to 4)

## Stand-Alone Romantic Suspense

- Never Gonna Happen

- One Hot Holiday
- Secret Admirer
- First Taste of Darkness
- Sinful Secrets
- Until Death
- Christmas With A Spy